Co...

1. – Blood on the Tarmac	1
2. – Many Happy Returns	15
3. – Cheek by Jowl	31
4. – When Rugby and Morris Meet	49
5. – A Handkerchief Too Many	61
6. – Follow Your Nose	81
7. – Albania to Albion	99
8. – Bus Rides and Blue Tape	109
9. – Long Shots and Long Snouts	121
10. – It All Comes Out In the Wash	131
11. – Circles and CGIs	139
12. – *Mirupafshim* and *Faleminderit*	149

Best Wishes

THE WHITBY DANCER

Pete Ardern

The Whitby Dancer
A Billy Ingham Adventure

Peter Ardern

JANUS PUBLISHING COMPANY
London, England

First published in Great Britain 2009
by Janus Publishing Company Ltd,
105–107 Gloucester Place,
London W1U 6BY

www.januspublishing.co.uk

Copyright © Peter Ardern 2009

British Library Cataloguing-in-Publication Data
A catalogue record for this book is available from the British Library

ISBN 978-1-85756-674-1

All rights reserved. No part of this publication may be reproduced, stored
in a retrieval system or transmitted in any form or by any means,
electric, mechanical, photocopying, recording or otherwise,
without the prior permission of the publisher.

The right of Peter Ardern to be identified as the author of this work
has been asserted by him in accordance with the Copyright, Designs
and Patents Act 1988.

Cover Design: Edwin Page

Printed and bound in Great Britain

1

Blood on the Tarmac

Billy came to in the ambulance. A medic was bent over him firing off questions.

"What's your name, sunshine? Can you hear me?"

Billy nodded wearily.

"Good lad. Can you tell me your name?"

"Ingham ... Billy ..."

"What's your phone number?"

Phone number? Billy was too stunned to work it out. The interior was spinning round and the back of his head was hurting like hell.

He lifted his hand; it was covered in congealed blood. He didn't know where he was or what he was doing. He just felt an overwhelming tiredness.

"Want to sleep ..."

But the man kept annoying him with questions, trying to keep him conscious.

"Billy! Billy can you hear me? Just give us your phone number."

Billy reached into the back of his mind. There was nothing there but a swirl of images and echoes. He blurted out a series of numbers automatically but it was too great an effort. He was being sucked into a black hole. There were people circling around trying to hold onto him, but he was falling ... falling ...

The next thing he knew he was on a hard bed caged by a metal frame. He could see a woman with dark, waist-length hair in the corner of his eye. Was it a witch?

She was stroking his hand and repeating, "It was meant to be ... meant to be ..."

Billy strained to get a better look at her. She tilted her head in sympathy.

"You'll soon be all right, love. I've brought you some pyjamas."
"Pyjamas?"
"They're going to keep you in overnight."

She melted into the background. A small, stiff woman in a pale blue uniform stepped forwards. She cupped her left hand under his neck, took a lint cloth out of a kidney-shaped bowl and began to bathe the wound on the back of his head. He flinched.

"Soon be done. Just clean it up then we'll glue you back together. Does he have any allergies?"

"I don't imagine so," a voice replied from somewhere. "He's as tough as old boots. Like me. I've had to be."

"Yes. Perhaps you could wait outside with the others just now?"

The woman was too busy for life stories. Her voice was flat and businesslike as she rummaged around the instrument tray, which made unbearably sharp tinny sounds.

She angled Billy towards her, so she could clip hair from around a deep gash. She plonked the scissors down and tore a handful of cotton wool from a packet. She began to dab and wipe, but Billy jerked back again.

"Just relax if you can."

She tossed the cotton wool onto the tray and reached for something out of sight, then began to work on him again. He felt an even more intensive sting, almost a burn as she applied surgical glue.

All the time the woman in the background was going on about an accident she'd had as a child, about good old-fashioned stitches and matrons with starched collars.

What's a witch doing in Levis? Billy kept wondering. Nothing made sense. He seemed to have woken up into another world.

The nurse was giving him a lecture on how to look after wounds, but he was already floating backwards into that deep, black chasm where sound was hollow and impossible to pinpoint ...

The screech and rattle of a lift opening woke him. He was being wheeled along a silent, half-lit corridor. A male nurse was on one side of him leaning forwards to guide the trolley and the strange lady was on the other side holding his hand. She was slightly stooped over, so that her gait was awkward and her lank hair hung to one side.

"We're going to X-ray. They say it's only a precaution ... it's got to be done. Then you'll be able to rest."

The rhythmic flashing of ceiling lights came to a stop. He swerved into a dark void. The voice was cut short by the soft-cushioned swish of a door.

A new face appeared out of the gloom. It was a middle-aged, bespectacled lady with a grand, lacquered hairdo, like someone off *Coronation Street*. Another face appeared – a younger, prettier girl.

She forced a smile and together with the man, they took hold of his useless limbs and slid him on to a cold metal surface. A set of lights swung across the room and hovered over him like a UFO.

Maybe he was being abducted; maybe it was all a bad dream. After a few seconds it flashed then the manhandling started again, followed by more flashing lights. The older woman gave a running commentary.

"Smile for the camera!" was the only thing he ever remembered.

After what seemed like an eternity he was spun out into the corridor, where the witch was waiting for him. She stroked his forehead with a clammy hand. He wanted to pull away but was too weak.

"They said you were always getting into scrapes! I thought they were exaggerating! I'll be here in the morning, love."

With that, he could hear distant voices and shoes tap-tapping 'til they were out of earshot. A door slammed shut. He was jolted into a lift. Sleep overwhelmed him again ...

He woke up in a ward of eight beds, four on each side. Some were partitioned by screens, others open to view. All were occupied by middle-aged men. Directly opposite him a patient was hidden under a tent-like sheet and connected to a complex of whirligig tubes. Every few seconds a muffled groan emerged from the heap of linen.

Sounds of a football match echoed down the corridor and Billy could hear spasmodic oohs! and aahs!

"We're one-nil down ... I said one-nil," someone shouted.

Things were starting to come back to him ... bits of memory stitching themselves together. Yes, of course, there was an England match. They were going to watch it after milking. They'd got done early, so they could see it. They weren't that much into soccer, Grandad and him, they were rugby nuts but it was a World Cup qualifier.

A rotund, ruddy-cheeked nurse glided into his bay as if on casters.

"Now then, 'ow's our little luvvy?" she said in a gruff, northern accent.

"Er ... Billy Ingham."

Billy was not used to being called 'luvvy' or 'little' for that matter.

He was a typical prop forward and a good two stone heavier than he should be at sixteen.

"'Ow are you? Not what's your name? You are in a state, aren't you?"

He'd slumped down the headboard since her last visit. She leant him forwards, plumped up the pillow behind him and reset him higher and a little to one side.

"Stay like that if you can, luvvy. Let the wound settle. Now, do you need anything? Are you in any pain?"

"I've got a headache ... feel dizzy ... chest hurts ..."

"Is that all? Ha! Ha! I'll check with the doctor and get you something. And I'll try and get you moved as well. You shouldn't really be in here with this lot. We're short of beds ... short of everything ..."

At that point, a large, tweedy figure lumbered into the open end of the ward. Even with half his wits missing Billy recognised him straight away.

"Billy! I've been to fetch a few more things for you. Your shaving gear and a change of clothes. Ha! Ha! Can't I even send you on an errand without you causing trouble for everyone?"

Just the sight of the bluff old man raised Billy's spirits.

"Grandad, what's going on?"

"More a case of what's coming off, lad! You were knocked off your bike."

"My bike ... is it ...?"

"Don't worry about that now, lad. I'll pick it up in the morning."

"I don't remember being on the bike."

"You're still a bit bewildered, that's why. They're keeping you in for twenty-four hours' observation. Nothing to worry about; just a precaution."

"Twenty-four hours? What happened?"

"We sent you into Threapton to get fish and chips. Your nan was weary from the church hall do. The plan was to settle down for the match with a tray. Course, you seemed to be taking ages and then we got the phone call. We came as soon as we heard ..."

"Yes ... the match ... I just don't remember anything else ..."

Blood on the Tarmac

"It was that daft young Worsley's girl. Parked outside the chippy she was. Just opened the door without looking."

"And I ran into it."

"Aye. You came off like a blessed acrobat. Luckily, you landed on your head ... Ha! There was a shop full of witnesses. Ah! Here he is now."

"Who?"

"The police. Want to strike while the iron's hot. They're always so damned busy these days even in Threapton."

A very tall, very bald PC strode into the ward. Grandad beckoned him over.

"Here he is – Evel Kinievel!"

The policeman took a pen from his lapel and looked down sideways at the patient. He scribbled a heading on his pad.

"OK if I ask you a few questions then? Are you up to it?"

It was soon clear Billy wasn't. He stared into space, while PC Kirk read through the background information. He might as well have been reading a bedtime story. "... and then you must have turned right at the junction of Threapton Lane and High Street, heading in the direction of the chip shop. Now, do you recall seeing a white Mini Cooper to your left?"

"No."

"A door being swung open in front of you?"

"Er ... no."

"The moment of impact, perhaps. How did that happen?"

It was hopeless. The cupboard was bare.

"Huh! I just don't know."

"So you weren't aware of the row of cars parked to your left?"

"I don't even remember being on my bike."

"As I feared; far too soon. You really do need a spot more recovery time."

Grandad was shaking his head in disbelief.

"You must remember something, Billy."

"Never mind, Mr Ingham. Fortunately, it's pretty straightforward. She's admitted everything. Of course, it is always nice to get it from the horse's mouth if we can. Maybe we can try again in a day or two, when you're feeling better. Then, how we proceed will depend on how far you want to pursue it."

The Whitby Dancer

"We don't want to make a fuss with charges," Grandad said on Billy's behalf.

"Well, maybe you don't, sir, but we do like to discourage such carelessness. She could do with a talking to at least. Could have killed him!" He tore a page off his note pad and handed it to Grandad across Billy's chest. "Her details. If I were you, Mr Ingham, I'd get a solicitor onto it. She shouldn't get off scot-free. It's something we see too much of ..."

They carried on discussing over him like they were bartering at a market stall. Billy shut his eyes and drew the sheets over his face. The doom-laden tones of a commentator echoed down the corridor.

An unshaven man limped in on crutches and started to rant,

"Would you credit that? Lost three-two to a tinpot excuse of a nation. We're out of it now. Get one hundred thousand quid a week to play like a bunch of nancies. Us lot could have done better. Even old Alan here!"

He slumped down onto the end of his bed. It was like the death scene in a tragedy. From Alan's bed, a skinny, shaky hand appeared from under the cover. It fumbled around 'til it alighted on the syringe at the end of a long tube. It gripped it and pressed down. Billy felt an irresistible urge to see if there was a person attached to the disembodied hand. He pushed back the folded-over sheet and levered himself up onto his elbows, but he caught his wound on the angle of the pillow. His eyes screwed up in agony.

The nurse came in at that very moment. Her ample backside protruding as she pushed along a mobile bureau. She left it in the centre of the room and stalked up and down the ward.

"I have to get on with the medication now. It's getting on for ten, so if you don't mind ..."

She wagged a finger at the policeman.

"We're about done, thank you. Let me know if anything crops up, Mr Ingham."

He snapped his notebook shut, reached across to shake Grandad's hand and without a word to Billy, lurched down the corridor. His heels squeaked on the shiny floor until he disappeared into the distance.

"You'll be all right here," Grandad said. "It's spotless. There's no record of MRSA at Shirlington," he added in an attempt to cheer Billy up. "I'll just find out what's to be done."

Blood on the Tarmac

The nurse heard him and shouted across, "Leave your number at the desk, Mr Ingham. As soon as we know ourselves, we'll let you know when to pick him up. And don't you be worrying. I'm sure he'll be as right as rain by tomorrow."

Billy desperately wanted to go home, but he was far too feeble to make a scene.

"I'll leave you to it, lad," Grandad said, patting him a bit too heartily on the shoulder.

"Ouch!"

"You're in the best place just now." He tipped his cap forward and scratched the back of his head. "I don't know. She's back and now this has to happen. You couldn't have timed it better, could you?"

Billy was still trying to picture himself somewhere on his bike in Threapton.

"We'll come for you as soon as they ring. We'll bring Twiggy. That'll cheer you up, eh? Maybe we'll get those fish and chips, too. Better late than never."

Twiggy? Fish and chips? The last thing Billy wanted was the dog jumping all over him or Edwards' soggy chips.

"Someone will have videoed the football. I'll ask round at The Thumb ..."

"I wouldn't bother if I were you, mate," the distraught man quipped from the other side of the ward. "Watch that and he'll have a relapse ..."

Grandad laughed and went over, intending to share a joke. He was that type. But the nurse was on the warpath and shooed him away. He responded like a kid caught scrumping apples.

"All right, I'm off! I'm off! See you tomorrow, Billy!"

He ambled out of the ward, nodding goodbyes as he passed.

Billy sank back into the pillow, this time with his head carefully angled to one side. An even deeper, longer groan came from the crumpled heap that was Alan. The nurse mimed a thumb motion towards him.

"Any time you want, press the button. That's it; press the button if it gets too much for you, my love."

She lingered by the drugs trolley gathering her thoughts. She checked the paperwork propped up between some containers and then peered over her bifocals at Billy. She rattled some tablets out of a box into a tiny plastic cup, which sounded rather like dice.

"Now then, the duty doctor said you could have some paracetamol for your headache."

But Billy had already been drawn into a deep, dreamless sleep ...

Hospitals are hell in the morning. The smooth functioning of the organisation comes before the comfort of the individual. A patient can be at death's door, but the daily routine must be observed.

Nurses have to get done. Shifts have to change. A ward is not exactly a restful place and staff are not obliged to put on a cheery aspect – they're part of a system, a process, a factory that copes, just copes with the main product: suffering. From the time of the Crimean War, when Florence Nightingale first introduced organised care, the routine was set in motion. It had super-concentrated over the years.

So, not long after dawn, Billy was woken. He watched in horror as the able bullied the helpless into life. He would prefer to manage by himself. He needed the loo, but was too proud to use the banana-shaped receptacle left on the swing tray beside him. He rolled to the edge of the bed and lay on his stomach. Then he stretched his right foot down onto the cold tiles and gingerly transferred his weight onto it. Already, his head was swimming and the pulse in his neck was throbbing. He eased around until both his feet were on the floor and his chest was flat on the mattress. As the dizziness subsided, his balance righted itself. He pushed himself up to the standing position and spun slowly round on his heels ready to go. But walking was another matter. Getting across a room was like climbing a mountain. He could only shuffle along, inch by inch, like a man with vertigo on a ledge. He focused on the distant WC stick-man and by sheer willpower, he made it to the row of doors at the end of the room. He made for the nearest cubicle and collapsed onto the freezing toilet rim. The smell of disinfectant and stale urine almost overwhelmed him.

It was half an hour before he climbed back into his bed, exhausted. Next time, he would have to use the cardboard thing.

He was beginning to feel more like himself, but there was a downside – the awareness of hunger and injury was growing. The pain in his neck was so severe he could hardly turn his head. The muscles at the top of his back, normally so strong through scrum training, felt as if they were ripped from the bone. He opened the top two buttons of his pyjama top. A symmetrical bruise ran the length of his chest. The top edge of the car door had engraved him with machine-like precision. He prodded it. It was burning tender. He was heartily sick of the whole experience. It was not yet six thirty.

At six fifty, a dapper young doctor breezed in with two student nurses, like a rock star with two groupies.

"Morning. Doctor Burridge. You are ..." He scanned his notes briskly. "Ingham. W. The RTA." He peeled back the cover and peered at the bruising on his chest. "Superficial. The X-ray revealed nothing ... and the back?"

Billy turned over.

"Ah! Not so bad. Tender?"

It was. He raced through a series of questions, at the same time ticking off a sheet of paper on a clipboard.

"So. Are we clear of the dizziness?"

"Yes ... well ... er ... sometimes I'm a bit –"

"Sometimes. No headache?"

"No."

"No blackouts?"

"No."

"Nausea?"

"Pardon?"

"Sickness?"

"No ..."

"Blurred vision?"

"No."

"Reflexes? Normal?"

"Normal."

"Goo-ood!" The doctor turned his attention to the nurses. "We shall do the routine tests, of course, but on the face of it everything indicates superficial damage only." He took a tiny torch from his top pocket and shone it into Billy's left eye. "He was lucky ... if there'd been any following traffic ..."

Billy didn't feel lucky. The doctor switched to the right eye and continued his lecture as if he wasn't there.

"The X-rays would indicate that there's no brain damage, no nasty little fractures or depressions ... twenty-four hours will be sufficient in this case." He had a final prod along the collarbone.

"Deep bruising here and here ... no complications ... sit up, please!" He placed his hands around Billy's temples. "Just try to turn your head, very slowly ... to the right ... good ... to the left ..."

Billy could only manage the tiniest movement either way.

"And up ... and down ... yes ... yes ... When it settles down, we'll know better. It's likely he has a whiplash type of injury. He'll need some physio, but he can sort that out with his GP." The doctor scribbled on his pad. "Discharge at three. See if you can get some breakfast down you ... er ... William. We'll give your parents a checklist of what to look out for. Just in case."

"Grandparents, Doctor."

Billy was always keen to let people know the real situation.

"Jolly good."

He ended his notes with an emphatic full stop. He signalled to the nurses and they drew the screen around the next bed mechanically.

"Ah! Mr Sutton, the Transco accident!"

Soon, Billy could hear the rustling of sheets and the cold, efficient voice.

"Collapsed lung. Severe contusions to the left chest ... no fractures ..."

Everyone was treated in exactly the same way. Within half an hour, the entire ward was done. The doctor swept out, his white coat billowing, the nurses chasing at his heels. The torpor returned.

At seven fifteen, the breakfast trolley trundled in. A grim-faced nurse served up too quickly, like an irritated dinner lady, and left them to it. No time to assist. Stan, the collapsed lung next door, offloaded his cereals and curly toast on Billy.

"I think they're trying to finish me off."

Billy's appetite was back. He could eat for England. He stacked the dishes and plates up precariously on the trolley and then wheeled it well away from the end of his bed.

Another hour passed in silence, apart from the odd groan or clacking of false teeth. The atmosphere was miraculously lifted by the arrival of the newsagent, a spotty lad with a cinema-style tray hanging from his neck. It seems a man can get off his deathbed for a glimpse of *The Sun*. Billy had no money to spend. No one had thought to leave him any and he was too shy to borrow. He just sat and stared into the abyss created by boredom and pain.

Blood on the Tarmac

At eight fifteen precisely, two ultra-efficient nurses glided in and drew the screens around Alan. They worked in absolute silence. After a few minutes, they slunk away like cat burglars. Alan groaned even more deeply than usual and the syringe button was pressed three times.

Stan was slumped in his bedside chair reading the sports page.

"See that, lad?" he said. "He's got his own. We call them the cyber-nurses. You don't want a visit from them …"

Billy was trying to read the headlines. It said something about 'Millionaires Eat Humble Pie'.

Stan eventually dozed off, gripping the paper. Billy never did get to flesh out the story.

Time dragged unbearably. He became aware he was wearing Grandad's pyjamas. God knows how he got into them. They hung off him loosely – he looked like an inmate in a concentration camp. He took out the neat pile of clothes from the bedside cabinet and drew his screen half round. He would get dressed. There was no one around to tell him not to. He leaned the back of his knees against the bed for support and slipped off the pyjamas. Then he shook loose the freshly ironed T-shirt and boxer shorts and slipped them on with ease. But when he tried to insert a foot into a trouser leg, he toppled over. He tried again, this time lying down as rigid as a plank. It was a virtual tug o' war, until one final hitch of the waistband got them on.

He slid off the bed and launched himself down the corridor towards the faint sound of TV in the day room. He sneaked an easy chair from between two snoozing patients and pushed it to a quiet corner.

Usually, Billy hated daytime TV, but today he was drawn to it. The stories about bombs in Iraq were somehow therapeutic. The parade of soaps and quizzes and car boot shows distracted him completely. He soon forgot where he was and who he was. Being mindless was far preferable to being propped up in a hard bed in comedy pyjamas watching Alan pump drugs.

It was not until *Small Town Gardens* that the TV spell was broken, when Grandad arrived in a whirlwind at the ward desk opposite the day room. He was still in muck-spattered work clothes and seemed unusually flustered. Billy's Head sports bag was slung over his shoulder.

"Oh, there you are! Thank God you're ready to go, lad. She tried to bring the blessed dog in. Can you imagine that? She said it was good

The Whitby Dancer

therapy and lots of places do it nowadays! Well I asked, and they don't here! I made her wait in the car."

Billy assumed he was grumbling about Nan.

"We'll have to get used to it for the time being. Can you manage this?"

He handed him the bag.

"Yes. I'm OK."

"Then I'll cut along and sort out the paperwork. I can't roam around in this state."

Billy sat forwards and rubbed the back of his neck. He still felt groggy.

"Get up, get out, get up, get out ..." he repeated like a mantra.

He pushed himself up so quickly he keeled over. Luckily, no one was paying attention. He would have to be more careful – they might keep him in another twenty-four hours. From now on, he would do everything in slow motion. While Grandad was organising the discharge, he picked his way to the ward as if he were treading on hot coals. He gathered up the pyjamas and washbag from the end of the bed and bundled them into the bag. No time for folding or fussing.

He took a last look at Alan. The nightmarish arm with bulging blue veins was dangling out of the bed, motionless. Billy took a deep breath and, moving as confidently as he could, headed slowly back towards Grandad at the desk.

"All sorted, Billy?"

Grandad took the bag off him with one hand and linked arms with the other. He broadcast a loud 'Thank you' to the nurses lounging around the office and then guided Billy far too firmly towards the lift.

"Whoa! You're going too fast," Billy said through gritted teeth.

"Sorry, Billy, I'm still a bit worked up. Shall I ask for a wheelchair?"

"No!"

A porter who looked exactly like Paul O'Grady was arriving with a bundle of laundry. Even in a state of agitation, Grandad saw the chance for a joke.

"Thank you, bellboy! Lingerie department, please."

"That's bad luck, I'm on the way to the morgue ... Can I do you for a shroud, sir?"

He even sounded like Paul O'Grady.

The sinking lift brought Billy's dizziness on again. He casually but grimly hung onto the support rail and joined in with the small talk as if everything was hunky-dory ...

"There you go! Compliments of the National Health Service!"

The porter let them out at the ground floor. Billy watched him through the cage door pinching the bridge of his nose and shouting, "Dive, dive, dive!" as he went down. Yes, he acted like Paul O'Grady, too.

They plodded along endless corridors, asking for directions several times, until the bright light of the main foyer appeared as a dot in the distance.

"The light at the end of the tunnel," Grandad said predictably.

"I've just picked your bike up on the way here. The bobby put it in the yard behind the chip shop. Bob Edwards was very helpful ..."

"Is it all right?"

"I'm afraid it's had it. It looks like it's come off worse than you. Anyway, we'll sort something out."

Billy imagined his BMX in a mangled heap of spokes and chrome.

"And you've left your mark, lad. There's an enormous blood stain on the tarmac. Bob picked this up as well ..."

He handed over a wallet. It was a holiday gift Dad bought in Corfu. It was good to see something familiar, even though it had a perfect fingerprint of blood on one side. He slid it into his jeans pocket, without checking the contents.

"You may have been half-dead, but you kept hold of your wallet!"

They emerged into the foyer. Elderly folk in wheelchairs, mothers with pushchairs, secretaries with files, porters, doctors, all careered round like they were in a giant pinball machine. Grandad sensed the lad was overwhelmed. He gripped his arm tightly. They zigzagged towards the automatic doors. It was a bright, sunny day and the air was fresh and crisp. Just to feel it on his face raised Billy's spirits. They stepped onto the covered walkway between the endless rows of cars.

"Row U ... couldn't get any closer. Sorry about that!"

Even from a distance, Grandad's battered Land Rover stood out from the more image-conscious models around it – four-wheel drives that had never seen a speck of honest dirt. It was a comforting sight after the night's traumas. Billy could already hear Twiggy yelping. He squinted to try to catch a glimpse of her. There was someone sitting in the front seat trying to keep her under control. As they drew closer, he

The Whitby Dancer

could see it certainly wasn't Nan. It was a pale-skinned lady with raven hair, streaked with hints of premature grey. She had a long, hooked nose and wire-rimmed spectacles ... and that tatty denim jacket ...

The awful truth dawned on him. Either he was hallucinating or it was Mother ...

2

Many Happy Returns

So you've had an accident, scarred the top of your head for life, stretched your neck like a rubber band, been so badly concussed you can hardly walk. Your brand new bike is wrecked, favourite T-shirt ripped to shreds, best jeans re-dyed with bletch and blood. Rugby training has become a distant dream. The holiday you planned with your best friend is scuppered. You can neither bike nor camp nor fish nor farm. It's the first week of the holiday and life has gone pear-shaped in one crazy second. Why? Because Tracy Dawn Worsley of Shirle Grove, Threapton, 18 years old, doing a BTEC in beauty therapy at Shirlington Tech, was answering her mobile instead of looking before she opens her car door. Answering her bloody mobile. What was that about comedy and timing?

The last thing Billy wanted as he staggered out of hospital was the sight of a mother who, four years before, had dumped him on his grandparents' doorstep. For she it was, who appeared at his bedside that fateful night. This was a tsunami crashing over his new and settled life, a life he preferred to anything that had gone before. He never even thought about his head-in-the-clouds mother or his money-grubbing father. 'Dysfunctional' was invented to describe them.

Fate being the trickster it is, at the very same time Billy was somersaulting over his handlebars, a bedraggled woman was arguing with a taxi driver at the end of Brandywell's long gravel drive. A shoulder bag and one suitcase were all she had. Nan had spotted her from the kitchen window and her heart missed a beat. Grandad had heard the commotion and rushed from the milking parlour to the front door. He paid the taxi driver off to the tune of twenty pounds, while Nan ushered her into the kitchen, sat her down and put the kettle on. They'd listened in horror to what she had to say. It seemed the 'celebrity chef' she ran off with had far more ambition than ability.

"Huh! He was more Gordon Bennett than Gordon Ramsay."

The Whitby Dancer

The truth was, he couldn't cook *un oeuf*, let alone run a gourmet restaurant. She had been treated as a mixture of skivvy and milch cow. She had lost everything, the last vestiges of the divorce settlement. To get home, she hitched a lift with a booze-cruise on their way back to Dover. Using the remaining credit on her last credit card, she bought a National Express ticket to Birmingham and then hitched again to Shirlington. Outside the decaying sixties bus terminal, she jumped the queue to get a taxi. She had no money to pay for it but was past caring.

"You hitch-hiked in this day and age?" Nan kept asking. That was more scandalous to her than leaving the partner.

There was no option. She would have to stay with them for a week or two. Her own parents were in no position to help. 'Daddy' was bankrupt and living on a rough estate in Shirlington with his former secretary. 'Mummy' was in a hospice, unloved and unvisited.

"Oh I'll get round to seeing them, but not just now ... I can't face them yet."

It seemed Brandywell was the only place in the world she could go. It was fortunate that Billy's father was off the scene, so there shouldn't be complications. He hadn't been to the farm since he 'borrowed' a carload of heirlooms. Hopefully, he wouldn't even find out the despised ex-wife was home. It was while discussing the practicalities of sleeping arrangements that the phone call had come from Bob Edwards.

"Your Billy's been knocked off his bike, John ... and his helmet was still in the pannier!"

Mother overheard the conversation.

"What was that? My William? Knocked off his bike? Today?"

This one big trauma drove out all the others. Despite the state she was in, she was first to the car door ... first at the hospital bedside ...

"A belated display of parental concern ..." Nan whispered in the stark white corridor.

"Guilt," replied Grandad.

Mother's eyes were fixed on the odd couple staggering towards them. Billy was much broader, taller and more rural-looking than when she left him. 'Yokel' was the word that sprang to mind. The night before she had only recognised him with prompting from the in-laws. It could have been anybody lying there.

"Heaven's above, William! What have they been feeding you on – growth hormones?"

She got out of the car to help him in and then plonked herself in the back seat tight up against him. She passed over the dog as you would a teddy bear. The dog looked as shocked as Billy and trembled as only terriers can.

They were soon reminded Mother was not shy about airing her emotions. She spoke to Billy in the same confessional manner as she had to Nan and Grandad the night before. From the hospital to Brandywell they had to endure every last detail of the French farce again.

"And I just pray you never sit in judgement on me, William. It can happen to anyone, can't it? Yes, I've made my mistakes ... perhaps I should never have left in the first place. But that's life, *c'est la vie*."

She didn't think to ask how Billy was until they were passing Bob Edwards' shop, wittily called Mr Chips. Grandad, like a tourist guide, slowed almost to a stop and pointed to a crescent of black blood that straddled the centre lane marking.

"Can you see it, Billy? That's where they scraped you up! See how far you flew? Good stuff, though, Ingham's."

On seeing a bit of himself printed on the road, Billy winced.

Mother reached around him and shielded his eyes with her long, heavily bejewelled fingers.

"As if he'd want to see that!"

"Mind my neck!"

"*Pauvre bête*. We're having a torrid time, aren't we?" She planted a scratchy kiss on his forehead. Billy was mortified. "What doesn't kill you makes you stronger, William. Believe me. I know!"

She tightened a hug on him, French-style. Twiggy snarled and snapped at her. She jolted back into her seat.

"You'll have to sort out that dog, William. She's so aggressive ... even for a terrier."

She straightened her jacket and slipped back into Mills and Boon mode. It seemed the chef had been doing more than just help 'Chantal' make beds. They were trying out a few of them as well. As they turned into the drive, Mother ended the sordid tale with a pledge.

"I promise I'm going to make things up to you, William. That's all that matters to me now."

They were words that filled Billy with dread.

* * *

The summer days drifted along aimlessly. It was late July. Mother showed no sign of moving on and Billy was missing out on the very best time of the year. He was tormented by sound – house martins nesting under the eaves, insects clattering on the windowpane, cattle lowing as they lumbered up the yard, vixens yelping in the dead of night. He should be out there harvesting, riding round on the tractor and taking Twiggy for long walks around the riverside meadows. He loved mowing around the standing stones, the Twelve Witches, and fishing the oxbow lake. All was tantalisingly close; all denied to him.

The best he could manage was a stroll around the farmyard and a few paces down the grass lane to the fields. No one had warned him that the worst part of a head injury was the effect on the legs. Twiggy was bursting with her usual manic energy. He did his best to exercise her, but there's only so much stimulation in chasing sticks and catching balls. She was a farm dog.

He held boredom at bay with games on the computer. He read *Angling Times* cover to cover, every article, every ad. If the long afternoon really dragged, he knelt on the wheelback chair in his bedroom and watched Grandad from the window struggling to do jobs that were usually his. He kept up his scrumming strength with bouts of wall pushing and squat thrusts.

Sometimes, he would open the storeroom cupboard at the top of the stairs, where the musty air reeked of history. He rifled through the family photos so many times, he knew the exact order ... Great-grandfather Stott at Tripoli, Cousin Ronnie Ingham on Llandudno Beach, Auntie Sarah's wedding at Kidderminster, Threapton RU Seconds circa 1982 ... He emptied the Quality Street tins full of medals, coins and knick-knacks, laid them out on the landing, tinkered for a while, and then put them back again.

Mother was always hovering around. They barely communicated.

The novelty of rediscovering a son was short-lived. They would pass on the stairs and not speak – each locked in their own world. She was already planning her next move, phoning around, re-establishing old contacts in the area. Whether it was because of the shame of her failed relationship or the shambles of her marriage, she did not once call the parents. She had been a spoilt, only child like Billy's dad. It was no wonder the two clashed. She was one of those over-optimistic types who breeze through life never really planning, never looking back. And she'd never held down a proper job. She only signed on at Jobcentre Plus in Shirlington because she needed to get the money. She dragged Billy along to back up her hard-luck story.

He typed a false CV for her on his computer. She said it was a dummy run, but kept printing off copies and sending them out. She borrowed some money off Nan to buy some outfits from Marks and Spencer and make-up from Boots, "So I can feel good about myself again."

It was miraculous how quickly she got over a broken heart. Every day she was more and more upbeat; every day Billy was more and more uneasy. He had grown to like his life at Brandywell. He had taken to the countryside naturally. Now, doubt was creeping in. Put bluntly, Mother could claim more with a child in tow.

If the days were difficult, the nights were impossible. Owing to his aching neck, he was propped up in a permanent sitting position. When the light went out, he was tortured by thoughts of upheaval. He imagined the moment of leaving the farm – a grey, rainy day, traipsing down the drive with all his worldly possessions in bin bags (just as he had when he'd arrived). Then moving in with Mother, probably into a Shirlington sink estate, with all the charm of a vast open prison. And how could he cope with Mother's mood-swings? And what about those spooky friends she used to have? He remembered them arriving for seances and 'readings'. Tea leaves, tarot cards, crystal balls, you name it, they read it. She was never satisfied with 'now', always hankering after some fantastic future. He didn't want to leave the farm. This was home now. He would rather run away. He dreaded her hare-brained schemes, worse still a partner's hare-brained schemes. It was a waking nightmare. Would Nan and Grandad really let him go? Hadn't he proved his worth around the farm? And despite all that trouble with the treasure-hunter the summer before, wasn't it his money that bailed them out? But then they were getting on in years, near to retirement, and he wasn't exactly earning his keep nowadays. They might be pleased to see the back of me, he thought. He just couldn't tell. Unlike Mother, he was naturally pessimistic.

Amongst all the gloom, the only ray of light turned out to be the accident. Ms Worsley admitted to everything – Jesty and Simpkins Ltd were all but unnecessary. For them, Reference 000/254Ing was easy money. It was a case of how much Billy would get, not if. That would depend on the medical report and that, in turn, would be compiled when the physiotherapy was over with. Compensation would be calculated down to the very last scratch of chrome. There may, unfortunately, be a deduction for contributory negligence – as Soames Jesty sardonically said, "Youth doesn't think it needs a helmet."

But it could still be a very tidy sum. Worth the investment of pain.

Three agonizing weeks after Mother's arrival, Billy came down to breakfast one Sunday morning. It had been one of those muggy July nights, with distant rumbles of thunder. He hadn't slept a wink. For the last hour, he'd been tormented by the muffled sound of Nan and Mother arguing in the scullery. They had never got on. From the very first meeting, Nan thought Corinne was fey, selfish and practically useless. She was more interested in the arts than farming. She was also full of non-Christian ideas. The tension in the house had been rising and Mother was always making barbed comments about Nan's 'control freakery' or 'do gooding'. But that morning, when Nan asked if she would like to go to the church service, she went too far.

"There's more chance of hell freezing over. Half the clergy's bent, the other half deluded." Then she laughed in a cruel and superior way. Nan could take no more.

When Billy came downstairs, the argument was put on hold. Nan was glaring into the mirror, flicking her hair to the side of her face.

She nervously pinned a silver fern brooch on to her navy blue jacket and pricked her thumb in the process. She kept some plasters in her handbag for emergencies, so she clicked the bag open and rooted round for them. Billy noticed her hands were shaking.

"Your breakfast's under the grill, Billy. I did shout you."

Billy hadn't heard that amongst the other shouting that was going on.

"You'll have to warm it up in the microwave."

Nan swept out without saying a proper goodbye. She would never normally be so curt.

He took the oven gloves dangling from the handle, slipped them on and then slid his breakfast from under the grill. It was lukewarm and fading fast, but he was too on edge to bother. He sat down at the farthest end of the long oak table. Mother was sipping coffee and staring grimly into the middle distance. Some gaudy leaflets were spread out in front of her.

"When people get old, they become less tolerant. Where was I supposed to go? Salvation Army?" She took another sip. "I don't think we can stay here much longer, William, even if we wanted to."

The word 'we' sent a chill down his spine. He shrank back into his upright chair and picked at a piece of bacon.

"Religious fanatic. She thinks she's Mother Teresa. She'll be giving me a breakdown."

There was a silence. Billy didn't want to start her off on one of her speeches.

"As if I'm suddenly going to 'see the light' after all I've been through ... if there was a God in heaven, I wouldn't be suffering like this ..." There was another long silence as she sipped and stared into space. "When's your appointment with the physio, William?" she said at last.

"Tomorrow morning."

"And how long will it go on for?"

"Dunno ... an hour?"

"No, silly! I mean how many times will you have to go? Months? Years?"

"Oh, the doctor said it depends on how bad the whiplash was. I think he said it'd take about four weeks –"

"Four weeks. Where would that take us to?" She counted forwards a few pages in her tiny pocket diary decorated with Van Gogh sunflowers. "Hey! That could just about fit in!"

Billy cringed. Was she planning for the move? Planning to end his days at Brandywell?

"Why do you want to know?"

"Well, you know I wanted to give you a treat to make up for the last few years ..."

"Oh that's all right, I'm sorted."

"I thought it would be a great idea for us to have a little holiday together, just you and me. No cantankerous old grandparents around."

Billy grimaced.

"Yes ... get to know one another better. You see, William, I'm not an ogre. I didn't want to leave you behind in England, but there was your education and your friends here and I did sound you out about it, didn't I? Me starting a new life, I mean, and how that would be better for all of us."

"Oh. Yeah! I remember that. I'm really OK."

"And you were always aware of the situation with Dad. It wasn't out of the blue, was it? I was always open with you."

"Always."

"It was just one of those things. God knows what she's been saying about me over the last four years."

"Nan? Nothing bad, honest."

"I hope she hasn't poisoned the well for us."

There was another long, gut-wrenching silence while she went to the stove and poured a top-up of stewed coffee. It looked like mud.

She drew up a stool near to him and started to flip through the pamphlets. Billy felt he had to say something.

"To be honest, I'm not sure if I can go on a holiday."

"Course you can. Best therapy going."

"It gets a bit busy in the summer ... grain harvest ... and ... er ... that –"

"Oh, please say you'll go, William. I can't go by myself. And you know you're not fit to work yet."

With that, she scooped up the pamphlets, shuffled them into a pile and ran upstairs. Twiggy, relieved that she was finally out of the way, jumped onto his lap.

"Holiday ... with her? At least she didn't say we were moving out, Twigs."

He gently encouraged the dog off his knee. He unbolted the scullery door to the yard, stretched and took a deep breath.

"Come on, girl. Fetch your ball."

He took the fox-head walking stick from the umbrella stand and hobbled sideways down the worn, sandstone step. He was determined that today he would at least make the second stile.

Billy was in the bedroom dithering about and rubbing his neck neurotically. Grandad was running late. He always was these days.

The appointment was for nine and it was nearly eight twenty. He flung open the latticed window and shouted down the time. It echoed across the yard. Grandad hurried over to the house as fast as a gammy leg would allow – the nervy Hereford bull had kicked him the evening before. Even the animals were picking up on the tension around the farm these days.

"It's me that needs the bloody physio!" he said, bursting in and throwing his cap on the draining board.

Many Happy Returns

He washed his hands with the speed of a surgeon between operations. Nan, in close attendance, passed him a towel. A change of clothes was draped ready over the back of a chair. He peeled off the boiler suit and stepped into his market-day tweeds in one transaction, like a triathlete. Nan handed him a bacon sandwich and a mug of tea cooled with water from the tap. Billy appeared at the door and she pushed him through the kitchen, thrusting an appointment card into his hand as he went. Grandad followed a few seconds after. He heaved himself into the Land Rover with a world-weary groan.

"Sooner we get you right the better."

As he started the engine, Nan came to the window.

"We'll sit down to a proper breakfast when you boys get home!"

It was eight thirty-five when they hit the Threapton bypass. The traffic on Mondays was always bad. They hardly moved.

"What is it about Monday mornings?" Grandad said. "Who are all these people?"

He only ever went into Shirlington for market days and to pick up DEFRA forms.

They arrived with only five minutes to go. The car park was full.

They circled and circled, until all decorum was lost. Grandad muscled into the last parking space ahead of a pinstriped and very annoyed hospital exec. They arrived at the outpatients' desk with seconds to spare, flummoxed and ratty with each other.

"Tell 'em to change it to Thursday afternoon, Billy! No bloody commuters ... and I can kill two birds with one stone."

They signed in and took a seat in the waiting area, and waited and waited ...

Luckily for Billy, there was a thick stack of magazines on a rickety coffee table nearby. Someone, somewhere along the line had donated a Rugby World. It was falling to bits and was years out of date, but it was rugby. Billy flipped through, picking out any bits about England forwards.

"Do you remember this one? Peter Winterbottom? 'We can't run but we're experienced'?"

Grandad didn't respond. He had already slipped into waiting-room mode. He just sat and stared into space, delivering one of his Tibetan yak herder tunes, part hum, part whistle. Several elderly patients arrived, sat down briefly and were called in before them. Signs of annoyance flashed across Grandad's face.

"Shouldn't have bothered with the rush, Billy. Every bugger else gets seen to first," he said and then whistled some more.

They must have been waiting for an hour, when at last a neat, square-shouldered Asian girl of about twenty-five breezed into the middle of the ring of seats. She hesitated a moment and then called out, "William Ingham? This way."

Billy flushed; she smiled and turned briskly. He struggled to catch up and then to keep up with her. She swerved into a long room beyond the help desk and beckoned him to follow. It was very like that hospital ward full of screened bays. Each had a chair and treatment bed. As he passed by, Billy saw moaning patients being wrestled into odd configurations by the physios, who were all abnormally cheerful.

"Right ... can I call you William?"

"It's Billy, please."

"Billy it is, then. If you'll just sit there a moment."

She speed-read the notes on a clipboard. Billy had come to realise hospitals run on clipboards.

"Would you mind slipping off your shirt?"

He tugged his polo shirt over his head, lingering for a split second to hide the merciless blush invading his face. She was very pretty.

She peered at his chest.

"There were no fractures."

"No."

"All soft tissue injury. Sometimes that's much worse. Bones knit together."

She asked about the accident, but Billy still could not explain how the damage was done.

"You were unconscious?"

"Yes. For about an hour."

"And you were kept in for?"

"Twenty-four hours."

She moved behind him and gently prodded the pink furrow that ran across his number two haircut. It was 5 centimetres long and shaped like a horseshoe.

"Does it bother you?"

"No."

"It would if you were a girl. They hate scars. Now, if you could very slowly look up. OK ... look down ..."

She took his head in her hands and turned him gently to the right.

"As far as you can ... extension not too bad ... near normal ..."

But when she tried the same trick the other way, he could barely turn at all.

"As far as you can go ..."

"That is as far as I can go."

"Ah! I see ..."

She went behind him and worked methodically down his neck, pressing hard where the muscle attached to the spine. Halfway down the shoulder blade, she pressed one final, excruciating time. Billy almost jumped out of his seat. Cold sweat was running down his temples.

"Yes, yes ... as I thought ... just here, where the trapezius meets the vertebra."

She turned his head a fraction to the left and then scribbled furiously on the clipboard. Billy was near to fainting. The dentist had nothing on this.

"Now, if you wouldn't mind lying face down on the couch for me ..."

She conducted him to the plastic-coated bed in the middle of the room. An oval-shaped aperture was cut out near one end. Billy thought about the holiday snap of Aunt Edwina he'd found. Her face was stuck through a comic backdrop – she was an Arab on a camel.

Meanwhile, a long piece of tissue was torn from an out-sized kitchen roll and spread along the entire length. The physio pierced it through at one end and then made a tear over the aperture.

"Now, if you can just lie down on your tummy ..."

Billy lay down gingerly, shuffled into position and poked his head through the hole. There was a long moment of suspense while he was left to peer at the tiles. Then, out of the blue, she set about the sore spot with what felt like a knuckle.

"Yes ... torn here ... and badly compacted here ... comfortable?"

Billy gave a muffled and not very convincing "Yes."

"I'll leave you for a second."

When she came back, Billy felt a small, hot towel being dropped.

It was deliciously soothing, but after few moments of bliss, she lifted it off. She massaged around, squeezing rolls of flesh and then running her fingers along his tight muscles. She could have been a faith healer, the effect was so magical.

"You'll be having plenty of this over the next few weeks. It feels like knotted rope."

She came to a sudden halt and instructed him to sit on the edge of the bed. He levered himself up, but had sweated so much the tissue paper had stuck to his front. He looked like a mummy. He peeled it off in acute embarrassment and the blush returned with a vengeance. It spread rapidly from his cheeks to his entire face, then to his ears, where it grew so intense he could hear his own heart beat.

She carried on unconcerned. "Right, if you can pop your shirt on again."

As he was dressing, she stood square in front of him and re-enacted what he'd done. It was like an exotic dance.

"Your neck was extended forwards, tearing the muscles here ... then the head was thrown backwards. You must have landed directly where the cut was ... just there ... but then the soft tissue here and here was compressed and this nerve was a little bit crushed, so we'll need to get you to work on this and this ..."

The bizarre variety show wasn't over. She took an articulated model of a skull from a corner shelf.

"The neck, you see, not only holds your head up, it protects your spinal cord as well. Every day, first thing and last thing, you need to open up these joints, so ..."

The skull reared backwards and a row of teeth gaped wide. It seemed to be mocking him, delighting in his misfortune. She moved it around like a ventriloquist's dummy to illustrate particular exercises, but by now his eyes were glazing over.

"Repeat each one six times, increasing the push a little every day."

He did his top buttons up mechanically and followed her to the desk opposite the double-door entrance. She peered over at an appointment book as the secretary angled it up for her to see better.

"Right. Next Monday, same time?"

"Er ... yes."

"Shirley will sort that out for you."

She glanced at her watch, bid him a hasty goodbye and rushed off to call in the next patient. Grandad was still perched on the edge of his chair with his cloth cap held in front of him. He hadn't moved in the last half-hour. He was in a trance.

Many Happy Returns

"Probably thinking about work," Billy said to the secretary behind the desk. "He's either working, or thinking about it."

"Like us," she replied, passing him the appointment card.

Grandad heard Billy's voice. "All done, lad? See, it wasn't anything to worry about, was it?"

Billy smiled and took out a sachet of Ibuprofen capsules.

When they got home, they draped their jackets over the backs of chairs carelessly and sat down at the long table. They said nothing for ages, just wallowing in the smell of fry-up drifting from the kitchen.

Grandad eventually came out with his favourite quote.

"The anticipation is greater than the event!"

Nan breezed in and started laying knives and forks just as the back door swung open. Twiggy yelped. It was Mother. She'd been into the village to pick up her special order magazines. No one spoke to her.

"And a good morning to you, too," she said sarcastically and made for the two A4 envelopes Nan had propped up on the mantelpiece.

"For me?"

"The one on the left." Nan replied coldly. "The other one's for Billy."

Mother went up to her room to open it in privacy. Ever since her marriage, she was fussy that way. Billy eyed the ominous, large brown envelope.

"No! No! Have your breakfast first, Billy!" Nan said, but he was already at the fireplace tearing along the top edge clumsily.

"Well, lad?"

"I'm not sure."

As he had feared, it was more confusing legal stuff. He passed it to Grandad to sort out.

"Ha! Worsley's insurance company has agreed liability."

"What does that mean?"

"It means they won't contest damages up to ten thousand. Of course, it depends on a medical examination 'with the recommended specialist given in the attached document'. Just practise a few disabilities, lad!"

He did a Quasimodo impersonation round the table.

"Now, now, John!" Nan said. She couldn't see the funny side.

He stopped and read the letter over again. Breakfast was temporarily forgotten.

"Look at this! Jesty's cut ... up to 2,000 ... for doing nowt! Should have been a solicitor myself. He was as thick as a farmhouse butty at school."

He passed the document to Nan. She read over it slowly with a frown, but at the same time nodding approval. She cast her mind back to the lightning strike of luck they'd had the year before, when the treasure trove had turned up on their land.

"It's an ill wind," she mused.

"Perhaps the accident's done you a good turn, Billy!"

Nan passed the letter back to Grandad and he returned it to Billy with a broad grin.

"You'll be able to pay us back for that damned holiday she's tapped us for."

There was a stunned silence. The bombshell had dropped.

"John! What did I tell you?"

At that moment, Mother flew downstairs, waving something triumphantly in the air.

"William ... they've arrived!"

"What?"

"Our tickets."

"Tickets?"

"Er, hello ... for our holiday?"

"For our what?"

"All-week tickets. They get you into anything you want: performances, workshops, ceilidhs the lot! Even covers the campsite if you need it."

The penny instantly dropped. As a boy, Billy had been taken to the Whitby Folk Week year after year, hoicked along like a rag doll. She was a folk nut long before it was back in fashion and folk nuts are creatures of habit. Dad had never gone with them. He preferred his annual 'time out'. Anyway, country and western night at The Miller's Thumb was the limit of his musical taste.

"It's going to be our special time together, just like the old days."

Grandad's eyes rolled to the ceiling in sympathetic horror.

A powerful flashback came over Billy. He is lying on a cold, hard groundsheet in a musty-smelling tent. Seagulls are squawking, the sea is roaring and banjos are twanging in nearby tents. Mother is attempting to sing *Little Matty Groves* in piercing screeches and yodels.

"Folk Week," he said distractedly. "... Folk Week ..."

"Yes, Whitby! Our favourite place! What do you say to that?" There was a long silence. "Well? Isn't it a lovely surprise for you?"

"Lovely? Yes ..."

He blurted out the exact opposite of what he felt. People often do when confronted with an unpalatable truth.

"The only thing is we haven't got a tent any more. Dad car-booted it after you'd gone." Billy was clutching at straws.

"No need. I've been in touch with Naomi. Do you remember Naomi Carpenter? We were such good friends ... she's letting us stay in her caravan."

Billy vaguely remembered a goofy, hale and hearty, Fair Isle sweater type, who reeked of stables and Fox's Glacier Mints.

"Or a car ... we haven't got a car."

"Oh, that's no problem!"

At this, Grandad and Nan cast sheepish glances at each other.

"Your Grandad's going to drop us off and they'll stay a night or two for a mini-break."

Billy couldn't believe they'd actually colluded in the idea and said nothing to warn him. Perhaps they were really planning to let him go altogether. This was just for starters.

"It will do you good, Billy. You need a holiday, time to get yourself right."

Nan spoke feebly. What she really meant was she needed a holiday from Corinne.

"But I'm fine now. Look, I can turn my head right round. And another thing, what about Twiggy?"

"You can take her with you. It's not a posh hotel, is it? And who's going to mind a dog at a folk festival? They're positively de rigueur."

Mother glowered over Twiggy, who was cowering in her wicker basket. She stooped and patted her head unconvincingly.

"And the best thing is, William, it's my birthday right in the middle of the festival."

Billy could see he was in a hopeless position. Of all the ways to recover from an accident, a week in a caravan at a folk festival with Mother was not one of them.

3

Cheek by Jowl

It was Friday the nineteenth of August. Breakfast was taken late to set them up for the journey. Billy was in his bedroom packing a holdall with all the enthusiasm of a soldier going to the front. Twiggy sat at the door watching his every move. She knew something was afoot and it wasn't the usual routine. The grandparents were in the next room mulling over what to take for a weekend break.

"Three pairs of trousers for two nights? Are you sure about that, Peg?"

Grandad emerged with two of the tartan suitcase set, the smallest one and the largest. He lumbered down the rickety staircase, bumping into the wall as he went. Nan, Billy and Twiggy followed him in silence. Mother was already waiting by the Land Rover. For the first time since her arrival, she was first up and full of beans.

Tyke Foster, Grandad's best mate from The Miller's Thumb, was busy hosing down the yard. He was stopping overnight for the next day's milking. Tyke and Johnny Ingham often helped each other out. No money changed hands. They paid in Witches Brew, the famous local tipple, and favours.

From the Midlands to the North, it was one unbroken wall of grey. As soon as they hit the coast road above Scarborough, rainstorms were rolling in off the North Sea. Layers of mud were shot-blasted off the side of the car. The Yorkshire countryside was too smudged, too indistinct to be enjoyed.

Mother decided it was a good time to share her knowledge of astrology. Everything, it seemed, was preordained. She clashed with Billy, because she was born on the cusp of Virgo and Leo, while Billy was a straight down the line Capricorn.

"You are an absolutely typical goat, William."

"A billy goat, I suppose," Grandad said.
"You see, it's the Leo in me that can't tolerate your cussedness."
"What's cussedness?" Billy asked.
"Stubbornness."
"I'm not stubborn."
"Huh! You certainly are."
"I'm not."
"See! That's it exactly. You prove my point. You just won't be told."

Billy dropped it to avoid escalation. Having pigeon-holed her son, she moved on to the in-laws.

"October, wasn't it, Peggy?"

How did she know that? Billy wondered. She hadn't sent a birthday card for years.

"Yes. The seventh."

"Wow. Absolutely slap bang in the middle!"

Nan was a Libra with brass knobs on. That explained her balanced and perhaps rather staid nature.

Nan kept her own counsel. She wasn't sure if she was being offended or praised.

Mother even worked out that Twiggy was probably a Scorpio.

"Why can't they have cosmic influences, too? Governed by Mars. That would explain her passionate and unpredictable nature. If any dog's got a sting in the tail, it's her."

Grandad was at his wit's end.

"Are you saying dogs have the same daft superstitions as humans? All she cares about is chasing rabbits and a regular chew stick! I hope we haven't got two days of this nonsense."

A couple of days? I've got a full week! Billy thought.

After three hours, they arrived on the moors just south of Whitby.

From a couple of miles out, they got a first spectacular sight, as panoramic as if they were coming down to land in a small aeroplane.

A jumble of tightly packed houses clung precariously to the steep sides of Eskdale. The harbour walls protruded into the thrashing sea like the claws of a giant scorpion. A brilliant shaft of light pierced the overbearing blanket of black cloud, lighting up the abbey ruins on the eastern cliffs high above the town. It was like an overdone fantasy filmset.

"See there, William? Those rocks under the Abbey cliffs? That's where Dracula came ashore."

For once, Mother said something that was vaguely interesting.

"Not the Dracula?"

"There is only the one," Grandad said. "Unless you put in for the job while you're here, Corinne."

"Huh! There speaks an archetypal bitter and twisted Pisces."

Billy sat forwards in his seat, dislodging Twiggy. Whitby, with the abbey glowering over it, did look considerably more interesting than the average seaside resort.

"Will we get chance to look round it?" he asked. "I mean those ruins?"

Grandad jumped in with a reply.

"Depends. They say Dracula charges an arm and a leg to get in ... Ha!"

Soon, any delight in getting there disappeared; they were quickly gridlocked into a traffic jam with hordes of arriving folkies and departing seafarers. A regatta had just finished. It took an hour to get into the town. Grandad, notoriously short-tempered in strange places, kept asking where the hell they were.

"You've got the bloody map! Oh, I forgot, females don't do maps!"

Mother and Nan were bickering.

"We've gone past it," Mother insisted.

"We haven't. Look – it's the next left."

"Turn!"

"How can I turn here?"

"Now you've gone and missed it."

"Huh. Bloody geography's what we want here, not astrology!"

For the best part of another agonising hour, they were sucked into and spat out of the heaving centre, each time getting more and more lost, more and more exasperated.

"See. Nothing's more stressful than a holiday," Grandad said.

Eventually, swinging between hot temper and cold desperation, he mounted the pavement on double yellow lines outside a newsagent. His 1987 AA handbook had proved hopelessly out of date – about as much use as a map of Narnia. He would have to fork out on a tourist map. On his way into the shop, he cast the well-thumbed manual into a bin with disgust. Billy watched two similar-looking men poring over a crisp, new, grossly overpriced map.

The Whitby Dancer

They quickly established that they were, in fact, a mere five minutes from the target: Clifftops Caravan Site. How they laughed.

But when Grandad got back in the car, he refused to answer any questions and accelerated off with an expression of grim acceptance.

They wound their way up a very minor road towards the abbey.

Before long, they arrived at the site. The newsagent was wrong. It was less than five minutes. The Carpenters' caravan was easy to locate, even for a man at the end of his tether. It was conveniently near to the washrooms and toilet facilities and it was also readily recognisable, being painted with shocking pink flowers on cream sides. Naomi Carpenter was of the same ilk as Mother.

"Nothing so stressful as a holiday," Grandad said for the umpteenth time as they pulled alongside. He usually avoided them like the plague. "They can destroy marriages, cause heart attacks. One little quibble ... a spoiled view, a dodgy meal, a trip on a 'Welcome' mat can lead to years of litigation. And if you want to find out what someone's really like, go on holiday with them."

As far as he was concerned, even the simplest holiday routine, say, unpacking a suitcase, causes the tension to rise and rage like a North Sea storm breaking on the harbour wall. Why? Because we all expect instant, sun-kissed happiness. But there is no solution to finding your way round an unfamiliar kitchen. And in a confined, unfathomed space, people bump into one another, they forget niceties. They even forget blood-ties, snapping and snarling like feral dogs.

It's like this: you just want to get on the beach, relax with your newspaper and your iced-cold drink, but you find yourself in a strange, uncontrolled world, with someone else's rules and regulations. A new world with no map, no compass and unhygienic toilets. And so it proved. Naomi's caravan was one three-dimensional plywood puzzle.

"Where's she keep the kettle, Corinne?"

"How should I know?"

"I thought you were a bloody psychic."

"For God's sake, use your own eyes."

"I bloody well would if I could find them. I just put them down and someone's moved them. Peggy, have you moved my specs?"

First major disaster: misplaced glasses. Second major disaster: no tea bags. A sigh welled up from Nan's deepest soul. She had forgotten to pack them; all she wanted was a cup of tea. Without that, she could easily have a nervous breakdown. She rummaged through every cupboard and alcove frantically. Corinne and Grandad had drifted into the lounge and were now arguing over the awning.

"It won't take five minutes."

"It's rotted."

"Wouldn't it be nice to sit out with friends?"

"What friends?"

"I know people here."

"You haven't been here for years! Look – it's a lot of mither over nothing ... have you seen the state of it?"

Grandad poked his finger through a hole that was obviously not one of the official variety.

"See?"

Billy had had enough. He scooped up the dog and made for the door. He slipped quietly down the steps. At a safe distance he put her down and took her lead from the side panel of his Trek and Trail body warmer. If a dog could ever look grateful, it was Twiggy now.

The clouds parted at last and though the north-east wind was chilling, the scene around them was inviting: rows of vans set in green meadows; purple moors forming an endless backdrop; people wafting away wasps and setting up picnic tables. He followed the metalled road between the caravans. Folk fans were arriving in their droves. Billy noticed several children with that relaxed, wind-blown look – the direct opposite of him. He had a solid, farmer-boy frame, bristly hair and prop forward shoulders. He sported an England Five Nations rugby shirt, 2006 and Fred Perry shorts. Cool. The shirt was already so worn the red rose was fading. Yes, it was going to be a lonely week.

After a few minutes they came to a junction where some shops and seaside stalls made a sort of shanty town centre. There was a signpost in the middle of the road, surrounded by a makeshift roundabout. Bedraggled bedding plants poked through drifts of sand.

Saltwick Bay ... the Abbey ... Whitby centre ... Cleveland Way ... He remembered Saltwick well enough. Once, Mother had skipped perilously close to the edge of the cliffs. She was doing her free spirit routine, communing with nature. His knees trembled just thinking about it. He shortened Twiggy's lead by wrapping it twice round his knuckles and drew her to heel. She was curious by nature. She had

The Whitby Dancer

recently tumbled into Threapton Park Lake in pursuit of a Canada goose. If she broke free here, she wouldn't even survive the fall.

They followed the signs for the Cleveland Way to the margins of the camp. Here, East Yorkshire accents filled the air. Tattooed blokes smoked fags, lummoxed on deckchairs and made postcard jokes.

Mothers bellowed at children to "Ger 'ere now!" or "Go t'goodie shop for me". He was reassured by the sound of normal people doing normal things. The kids were uncomplicated, more like the ones from school.

Within a few paces of the last caravan they were on the coastal path. The first sight took his breath away. Sheer cliffs tumbled into the surf and the path, riven with cracks, dipped down with the sweep of the land. Billy looked out to sea. Only a flimsy fence separated them from the perpendicular drop. Though the sky was now blue and the day calm, the swell still bobbed boats up and down like toys.

Distant tankers heading for the north-east ports looked ghostly in the sea mist. A pleasure craft got up as a pirate ship passed by the wreck of a fishing boat. Anyone who bothered to notice would quickly realise this coastline was no theme park. Fulmar squawked and gulls heckled on their ledges, hanging on to life by a thread. Yet immediately behind this dramatic and dangerous seascape, corn buntings and swallows swooped over peaceful meadows. The spectacular and the mundane sat cheek by jowl!

Where these two opposing worlds collided there was, logically, much more to see. It was a place that was teeming with life, a place where Billy could forget about the folk festival and be himself. He would come up here every day, even just for the odd hour. He was so taken by the surroundings he walked along airily, barely noticing the path under his feet.

Some 200 paces on, he came across a broken-down stretch of wall. He sat down, all the time looking around him. Twiggy scrambled up by his side. He took a plastic case from out of the zip-up side pocket. It was the small but high-strength binoculars Grandad had bought him from Oundle's Garage. They sat for hours taking it all in. While he watched and checked his pocket book of British birds, Twiggy luxuriated in the strange scents of a new place.

A distant chime of bells from the dale caught Billy's attention. It was five o'clock, Nan's rigid time for tea. Mother would be livid – she was going to the first concert at seven. Billy tugged some burr from Twiggy's Brillo Pad coat and set off in the direction of the abbey ruins. They could take the 199 steps that spiralled down into the town. A slow-paced circuit would get them back just a few minutes late, but late enough to avoid the usual mayhem.

The early evening sun burned hot on his neck, so he turned up the ample collar of his shirt. He looked back for a last time. Every now and then a stretch of land had slumped into the sea and the fence was pegged back further. Farmland was being steadily hewn away.

By the time Billy got back, the family were already eating yogurts.

His cheese salad was standing on the kitchen worktop covered in cling film.

"William, you were told to be back here for five sharp."

"It's only half past, Mother. I saw something really weird up in the meadows. That's what held me up."

"You and your meadows. We're at a folk festival now, not on a nature ramble."

"But it was really odd."

Grandad loved a yarn, especially if it annoyed Corinne.

"Well, go on, Billy! Don't worry, there's loads of time. I'll run you down if need be."

Mother scowled. She was snookered.

"On the way back up we came to a field behind the Abbey Museum. It was full of ponies, rough ones. I saw an old man leaning over a gate. I think he was a gypsy ... he was a bit like the Rogers in Threapton. He called them over, took a cigarette out of the packet, broke it up ... and fed it to one of them! As the rest came up, he did the same thing. Gave them a cigarette each!"

"That brings back memories. Don't you know what he was doing?"

"He's asking you, isn't he? For God's sake, get on with it," Mother said, tapping her wristwatch.

"All right! All right! Baccy – that's how they used to kill worms, see." Grandad was well versed in the old country ways. "And very effective it was, too! And they say the stuff's bad for you."

Billy was bemused.

"Nicotine, see. They use it in insecticides now. We didn't know that then, of course, only that it worked. And if it worked we did it."

The Whitby Dancer

"He'd love it if I let him smoke a pipe again!" Nan said, starting to tidy things away.

Mother was getting more and more agitated.

"William, can we please get a move on? Giving cigarettes to horses – I call that animal abuse. You'd tell him anything."

"I tell him the truth. Different from some folks round here."

Billy wished he'd never opened his mouth. He wolfed down the meal too quickly to enjoy it, passing over bits of crockery as he finished with them. Mother kept looking at her wristwatch and tut-tutting in Billy's direction.

"You'll have to do without a pudding, William. It starts at seven thirty and I don't want to miss anything. I've been looking forward to this for ages."

With that, she flew into her box bedroom next to Billy's at the end of the van and touched up her lipstick and mascara a final time.

Then she brushed her long raven hair, gathering it into a ponytail.

She looked like a Bollywood actress who'd seen better days.

"It's my time now," she said as she stared into the wardrobe mirror.

She swirled her skirt around several times. It was the same image she had perfected all those years ago when Threapton Folk Club was her only outlet. It was a world that was coming back into fashion. It said so in *The Times Magazine* she'd picked up on the ferry coming into Dover. Things go in circles. It was at that very moment she promised herself a new start, doing the things she wanted, when she wanted. No more being dictated to by men. Men! Was their sole aim in life to crush her spirit? She was the sensitive, spiritually aware type.

One disastrous marriage and one failed elopement were enough.

"It's time to live for 'me'. No more waiting on; no more spoiled dreams. World – here I come!"

She gathered up the ethnic shoulder bag she'd bought from Jade in Shirlington and breezed down the corridor practising a confident walk. Billy was opening a tin of dog food as she flounced into the room.

"William! You are not going dressed as a bloody football vandal!"

"It's a rugby shirt, not football. Rugby doesn't do vandals."

"Be quick and don't answer me back. I want to get a good seat. My favourite band's on first: Green Machine."

"That's a stupid name."

"I think it's a very clever name. They're Irish."

Billy remembered her liking for Irish jigs.

"It's like jazz. It all sounds the same after a while," he said forlornly.

When she added it was an all-Irish night, his heart sank further.

"They've got Colum Fitzgerald on fiddle and Tag Brady on whistle, and ..."

She droned on and on in folk expert mode. It wasn't her favourite band at all. She had simply mugged up on the programme, so she could impress people later.

She waited edgily at the steps while Billy threw on a clean T-shirt and his only jeans – the ones permanently stained with slurry.

"And, by the way, don't think you're going to wear that tatty body warmer thing. They'll think you're a gamekeeper."

Before long, they were slaloming down the church steps into town. Mother raced ahead to beat the swing bridge over the Esk and then hurried him alongside the harbour. Even the steep stairway up to the Captain Cook Monument didn't slow her down. Mother had conveniently forgotten that Billy was still groggy from the accident.

He could hardly keep up.

"William, please, it's another half-mile!"

She was fuelled by neat adrenalin. This was her first night out in three years. She kept checking the centre-page map as they scurried along in agitated silence – along the North Promenade, through the neat corporation flower beds, past the crescent and into the ordinary streets, well away from the sea front. At last, she came to a halt in the car park nearby a large terraced house, converted somewhere along the line into a public building. An old-fashioned sign outside said The Rifle Club.

There isn't really a word in the English language to describe how Billy felt when he eventually caught up with her, looked up and computed just where they were going.

"A folk concert, here? At a rifle club? And you wouldn't let me wear my body warmer? Dur!"

"William I hate that expression – don't you dare 'dur' at me!"

A handful of folk types were already queuing up outside the entrance. Billy quickly deduced they must be from the extreme nerdy wing of the folk movement.

"What a bunch of saddos ... dur ... the place isn't even open!"

"I warned you – if you're going to be rude, I shall ..."

The Whitby Dancer

Mother didn't have time to finish the sentence. A battered white van pulled up and three official helpers, all with baggy shorts and garish yellow 'Whitby Folk Week' T-shirts, got out. They took several cardboard boxes out of the back and swaggered up the steps importantly. Mother was holding the all-week tickets in her hand for all to see. In double quick time, they set up a folding desk, plonked down a pile of spare tickets and unlocked a pillar-box-red cash box.

Mother smugly stepped out of the line and proffered the tickets.

Billy, embarrassed by such forwardness, followed sheepishly. They were nodded through.

"Huh. They didn't seem very friendly. Used to get a warm welcome everywhere you went."

They squeezed up a dingy, narrow staircase into an upstairs social room. It was more suited to a domino knockout than a concert. The air was stuffy even before the room was full.

Regimented rows of plastic chairs were packed closely, too closely for someone of Billy's proportions. Mother, typically, made for the most central, most claustrophobic spot three rows from the front. When he sat down, Billy's thick prop thighs and broad shoulders overhung the seats on either side. He sighed. It wasn't difficult to predict the night ahead.

The place soon filled up. Mother kept looking round in childish excitement. A metal roll shutter suddenly clattered up at the back of the room. The bar was open. Mother stood up and draped her crocheted turquoise shawl on the back of her seat.

"What would you like to drink, William?"

She had dreamt of this moment for four years – her first pint of Guinness. She never really liked the stuff, but it went with the territory. Billy asked for a small shandy. As she side-winded off, the band was coming in. They looked suspiciously like students. They filtered onto the low stage, apparently made from wooden crates, where a forest of instruments already stood on racks. They did their final checks, plugged things in, plugged things out, placed things ready and then disappeared. The lead singer stayed back. He tapped the mic and flicked his foppish Hugh Grant hair a few times.

"One two ... one two ... one two ... one ... bit more bass, Jamie."

He jumped off the stage and retreated to the wings. The place was almost full. Billy looked around to see where Mother was. She was joshing with someone at the bar, probably about the Guinness. He was one of the stewards who had come in the van – an obvious musician-type with the hair and the attitude, but older, larger and sweatier. Eventually, she zigzagged down the teeming gangway and into their row, tripping over someone's desert boot theatrically.

Several disgruntled fans were forced to stand up and lean back.

She got to her seat just in time – the MC was stepping up to the mic from out of the melee. The MC was petite, fine-boned and dressed in a fusion of gypsy and Laura Ashley – a classic beauty once, but now too reliant on lipstick and eyeliner. She radiated a saintly smile and calmed the audience down with the hypnotic motion of her hands. Her voice was gentle and sing-songy and hinted she might be a performer herself. It all added up to a sort of faded charisma.

Mother scanned the programme intently.

"Esme McGarrigle. Thought so."

Esme McGarrigle welcomed everyone to this year's festival.

"We're destined to be the best ever; so many exciting young acts are coming to the fore." She ad-libbed painfully, while checking behind her to see if the band was ready. "So! What a treat to start us off on the very first night! All I really need to say is ... well, here they are ... Dublin's foinest ... The Green Machine!"

Applause cascaded through the room. The band stepped up, waved their appreciation, smiled broadly and jostled into position.

"Thank you, Esme! We're Green Machine and the first song is *Drogheda*. It's a song I wrote myself. You may have heard it on our latest album. *Green Men and Gremlins...*"

They took a moment to get psyched up. The lead singer ran his fingers through his hair a final time, stroked a plectrum gracefully across the strings of his guitar and then eased into a ponderous, dark ballad. It was about a brave rebel, hopelessly charging Oliver Cromwell's massed ranks on a faithful steed. Billy caught the odd bit: death of said faithful steed, bereaved colleen, shamrock lain on a bloody breast ...

The audience loved it. They clapped until their Anglo-Saxon palms stung. How time forgives. As the applause petered out, the band changed position and swapped instruments, ready for the next song. It began as slow as a dirge but gradually built up speed with the relentless Everton-Liverpool-Everton-Liverpool beat of the bodhrán.

The Whitby Dancer

The audience responded by drumming their feet faster and faster.

The flimsy linoed floor started to vibrate and Billy felt himself being bounced up and down. He imagined the floor collapsing and seventy beer-swelled folkies landing on an over-sixties darts team directly below.

It ended in a complete frenzy. The musicians had played themselves to a standstill. The audience, probably accountants, teachers and IT consultants, stood there wild-eyed and emotionally drained, as if they'd just been through the battle of Drogheda themselves.

Indeed, Green Machine was expert at toying with emotions. The next tune was a melodic harp solo played by the red-headed girl in the long green dress. The atmosphere became serene and thoughtful. After a second lilting air, played on fiddle and whistle, it was positively dreamlike. Mother closed her eyes and drifted away.

"I'm in another place, William ..."

"I wish I was," Billy said under his breath.

From then on, it was a relentless upping of the ante to the interval. The very last tune was *The Devil and the Drunk*, another jig that accelerated from nought to seventy and then ended at full pelt, like a train hitting the buffers. After an ecstatic applause, the lead singer stepped forwards, holding aloft a pint glass.

"Thank you ... thank you ... time to refuel ... time to worship the God of alcohol ... see you in fifteen ..."

Almost as soon as they were off the stage, Mother was on her feet.

She turned to go to the bar again. When she reached the end of the row she called back.

"Oh! Another drink, William?"

"Fizzy orange, please ... a pint."

He desperately needed fluids. Sweat was rolling down his temples.

Dishwater would have done. But it was a drink that Billy was never to get. The large, yellow, bushy-haired man was at the bar, exactly where he had been when Mother first spoke to him. He'd been watching the performance from the back with an air of superiority.

As Mother brushed past, he happened to shift on the spot. He stepped on her foot. She hopped on one leg. He apologised profusely. She said it was all right. He said he knew the perfect cure.

He delved into his pocket. She took off her shoe. He offered to buy her a brandy and lemon. She rubbed her big toe ... and accepted.

They got on like a house on fire. That's how life is. You have a disastrous year. You are lonely, low in confidence. So to cheer yourself up, you go to a folk festival, one you hadn't been to for years. At the very first concert, you simply stand at a bar and someone stands on your foot. Someone like you, who is a free spirit. Someone like you, who loves the music but who wants to let their hair down, not just sit there with the purists, the anals, holding it all in for the sake of decorum.

"Music's a heart thing, not a head thing," the man at the bar said sagely.

That was the moment Corinne Ingham knew, after five years of loneliness and failure, she had landed on her feet. Or, at least, someone else had landed on her feet. Within seconds, Terry Thwaites was offering Corinne a roll-up. Smoking was not allowed. In these deep green circles it was particularly frowned on. People would be very quick to complain – in a polite folky way – but they would.

"It's all so PC these days. Bloody stupid law. Used to smoke joints in these concerts, me! Not a problem."

"God, you're so right."

"Will you join me round the back?"

Corinne agreed, even though she'd given up smoking years ago.

But it was a way to keep the conversation going until she found out what Terry Thwaites was all about. She had a sneaking suspicion he might be a Taurus. He had those gigantic, bovine eyes. A dead giveaway.

Billy craned his head round just as they were slipping out of the fire exit. What should he do? Big as he was, he was far too shy to disturb anyone. He could see his orangeade on the bar going less bubbly by the second. He desperately needed a drink, desperately needed to stretch his legs. They were cramping worse than in a late-match scrum. But it was too late. The group was skipping onto the stage like fawns. He looked round a last time. The drink was flat.

Mother was nowhere to be seen.

It wasn't until Green Machine had finished their second set that she returned. Billy was angry, dehydrated, punch-drunk with reels and crippled by cramp. In the maelstrom of wild applause, blokes jostling to get near the bar, ladies jostling to get near the band, Mother slipped back along the row.

"Sorry about that, William. We couldn't get back in and had to wait at the door. You know what folk concerts are like. I bumped into an old friend, Terry."

Billy knew it was nothing to do with old friends or the conventions of a folk concert. It had taken her no more than six weeks back in England to find herself a replacement man.

"I had a feeling I'd meet someone. Didn't I mention Venus was in Leo right now?" Terry was milling around in the background as Mother spoke. "Anyway, he's heading off to the main venue to see Tinker's Cuss."

"You go with him, Mother. I'll be all right."

"Well no, William. I shan't leave you here by yourself. The next act's really good. We're going to team up later at the ceilidh."

"We're going where?"

"When I say we, I mean me and Terry. You won't want to go to a ceilidh, will you? It's dancing and stuff and I know that's not your style. I'll make sure you get home after this and then you can let them know I'm going to be a bit late." Billy nodded his agreement.

"Twiggy'll want attending to anyway."

She didn't usually trouble herself with canine care. She went to the bar, firmed things up with Terry then returned somewhat flushed to her seat.

"That's sorted, then."

The second interval was almost over; the posturing of the crew signalled the next band was ready. Esme McGarrigle, formerly of Elsinore, The Foot-tappers and Scrawny Dog (Terry's own in-house band, it later emerged) stepped up to the mic. She called the room to order with her Delia Smith impersonation.

"Cam orn ... let's be 'avin' you! Let's be 'avin' you! I wanna 'ear you!" She flipped from posh to Irish to Delia with amazing facility.

The Shenanigans were pretty much like the first band, except more gnarled and well-used in appearance. They came from Manchester, but all had Irish-sounding names, like Sean or Siobhan.

Their set vibrated along to the beat of the bodhrán as the audience went through the familiar Celtic mood swings, from frenzy to wistfulness. By the time Esme was winding matters up, thanking one and all to the high heavens, Mother was itching to get away.

"Come on, William. We don't want you to be too late home."

She grabbed the crook of his arm and ran down the steps of the narrow corridor before anyone could block it. They came out into harsh reality: traffic noise, drunken lads scrapping and girls baring their backsides to the world. Welcome back to England. She sped along the main promenade in silence. She frogmarched him past the Captain Cook Monument, through the upended whale's jawbone (the most surreal landmark of a surreal landscape), then hurtled down the cliff-hugging steps into the valley whimsically called by the locals the Khyber Pass. From there, it was another breakneck race along the harbour to the Esk crossing. And still not one word was spoken.

Only when they arrived at the bridge barrier, did she finally slow down and declare, "You'll be all right from here, won't you, love?"

"Course I will. I do have my memory back, you know."

"Then you won't forget to tell them I won't be late!"

With that, she was off to the Pavilion, already with the hint of a jig in her step.

Billy set off across the narrow bridge, stepping off the pavement several times to avoid revellers and strolling couples. He decided to take the old steps up to St Mary's Church and then walk around the Abbey Plain, rather than take the easier but less spectacular incline through the town. As he ascended, pushing his hands onto the top of his knees to help him, the distant Friday night sounds drifted up from the town. He felt he was an outsider, banished from the party that was going on all around him. But he was free.

When he got back, Nan and Grandad were still up watching *News 24* on the portable television. It was a vain attempt to replicate their radio habit. It was still not eleven o'clock. Twiggy jumped up and down, nipping at his cuffs.

"Mother's gone to a dance thing … a kali …"

"A what?"

"Oh, I dunno. She's with some friends; she won't be too late but says don't stay up or anything."

"I'll leave her a sandwich," Nan said.

"Come on, Twigs …"

"Good lad," Grandad said without looking round.

"There's a bomb gone off in Egypt. Some embassy or other. Thanks for that, Mister Blair. Don't go too far."

"I'm only going up to the church and back, not Cairo."

The Whitby Dancer

"Take a polythene bag with you," Nan reminded him. "I've left some on the kitchen table … special ones from ASDA. It's not like the farm here."

Soon, they were on the site road to the cliffs. The moon hung as low and as big as a Chinese lantern, what Grandad would call a 'harvest moon'. There was no need for his torch. It was uncannily still and the sea was as smooth as glass. Even Twiggy was becalmed by the atmosphere, but he still kept her on the lead. A free-spirited farm dog in a strange place is not a good idea. She pulled him towards every scent or scrap on the path until they came to the long wall at the back of the abbey, a stone's throw from Saint Mary's Church. As they squeezed through the kissing-gate entrance to the graveyard, she stopped, stood bolt still and cocked her head to one side. She raised a front paw, a sure sign that she had cottoned on to something.

She set off again pulling ever harder, eager to investigate. Billy could only see the long shadows of the church, pitch-black corners, where no moonlight penetrated, but he could hear a distinct scuffling. Twiggy started to growl. Billy picked her up and closed his hand round her mouth.

"Hush, girl …"

A small figure in a white top, luminous in the pale light, shot out from the church door and raced to a seat on the cliff top. It slumped down, head in hands. Billy gasped – he thought it was a ghost. He stepped off the path and ducked behind the nearest tombstone.

Twiggy squirmed as his grip tightened. He could just see over the elaborate gothic stonework. Faint sobbing suggested it must be a girl, a young girl catching her breath. Within seconds another figure appeared. It towered over her, slowly bent down and began to mutter in a low, agitated voice. It seemed to be enveloping her – the white all but disappeared. Half-lifted, half-encouraged, the girl was made to stand up. She clasped her hands together and shrank into herself as if not wanting to be touched. The sobs turned into cries, but with a forceful kind of sympathy, the dark figure conducted her towards the church. She was pleading and trying to pull free. They stood at the top of the steps for a second, silhouetted against the moon, then fell out of sight. But Billy could hear words carrying on the still night air; words he did not understand.

"Kur, Luan? Kur? Kur?"

He set Twiggy down and raced to the top of the steps. The two, still tightly entwined, were struggling at the very bottom. They turned sharply at the corner by the tea shop and were gone ...

That night, Billy could barely sleep. He was thinking about his mother, her latest friend and about the ghostly figures he'd seen by Saint Mary's.

4

When Rugby and Morris Meet

It was Billy's most uncomfortable night since the accident. The grandparents were already pottering about, making tea and ordering Twiggy around, exactly as they would at home. Grandad rang Tyke Foster at five to see if he'd started milking yet. In truth, after one night away, he was ready for home.

Billy decided to get up; there was little point in lounging around in discomfort. Mother had sneaked in at three o'clock like a wayward youth. It didn't go unnoticed, but who could say anything? She was a mature woman, wasn't she?

Billy emerged from his sparse box room stiff and bleary-eyed, exchanged knowing glances with Nan then sat at the rounded end of the formica-topped table. The lounge was flooded with blinding early morning light. That didn't help. Neither did it help when Twiggy jumped onto his lap to nuzzle his nose. Watching him eat at close quarters was her favourite pastime – she could usually cadge a twirl of bacon rind or a burnt corner of toast.

Nan was mulling over the day's activities – anything that did not involve festivals or regattas. She was reading a pamphlet in the manner of Judith Chalmers.

"Linger awhile in Grape Lane, where you will find the Captain Cook Museum and many antique shops ... antique shops, John! Many!"

She was a collector of Royal Doulton. Maybe she would treat herself to a pottery pirate or a fisherman, even a Captain Cook if such a thing existed. Grandad agreed tacitly with a nod of the head. He could just about endure the shopping as long as it was followed by a portion of Whitby fish straight off a trawler.

Billy washed up his dishes and dried his hands on his jeans. He slipped the dog's lead on while she was distracted by a piece of rind. It was a pristine, glowing morning, unspoilt by traffic noise. The only

The Whitby Dancer

noticeable sounds were the cry of seagulls and the distant wash of the sea. Billy took the same route he had the night before. He lingered by the seat where he had seen the girl. He kept checking the horizon, half expecting her to show up again. Twiggy circled round, snuffling at the plastic bottles, sweet wrappings and fag ends dropped by carefree tourists.

When he got back, the grandparents were gone, even though nothing would yet be open. A scribbled note was left on the lounge table, weighed down by a mug of cold tea:

> Billy, Corinne. Meet us by the monnument at twelve for lunch. We're doing the tat-shops and mewseums ... (Grandad was a rustic speller) then off down to the harbur to see the fishing boats go out. Love, G and N.

Boats going out? Billy wondered. Grandad liked to see how other men worked, so he could compare their lot with the lot of the farmer.

That was holiday enough to him. Mother was not yet up, but Billy could hear her stirring and yawning operatically.

She called out feebly, "William? Is that you, William?"

"No it's Count Dracula ..."

"Spare me the Ingham wit at this time in the morning."

"I'm off out now ..."

"Just come in here a minute, love ... and can you bring me a glass of water?"

Billy swilled a glass clean and filled it to the brim. Twiggy ran ahead and pushed the door open with her nose.

"Don't let the dog in!"

It was too late. Twiggy jumped onto the bed and licked Mother's hung-over face riotously. Billy dragged her off with his free hand and wrestled her out of the door. He placed the glass on the sill nearby.

Half the water was spilled.

"You really must do something about her! I'm soaked."

She struggled to sit up. The rings round her eyes were blue – you'd think she'd done six rounds with Ricky Hatton.

"Listen, love, I've made a very nice friend here –"

"Terry."

"Yes. He's really nice and very interesting –"

When Rugby and Morris Meet

"He looked interesting ..."

"Yes, and do you know, he actually lives in Whitby. Isn't that funny?"

"Well, not really. Someone's got to live here."

"You're starting to sound like Grandad. He moved here because of the festival oddly enough."

"But it's only on for a few days a year."

"Well, he based himself here because of his interests ... the folk scene ... he used to have his own group ... and the dancing."

"Dancing?"

"He's a morris dancer. In fact, he's started his own side. They call it 'side', love, not 'team' or 'troupe'. It came from nowhere, apparently. Now it's one of the best in the country. They win competitions all over the place, and ..." She sipped some water and brushed a lank strand of hair from her face.

"And?"

"And, my love, as it happens, he's quite a big noise in the festival ... helps to run it."

Billy had already worked that out.

"Did you notice his T-shirt?"

He had, but only because of the size of the stomach inside it.

"Well, it said 'Head Steward', and not only that, he's running a workshop."

Billy had always understood workshop was to do with 'work', like woodwork or metalwork.

"And I've signed us up for it."

"Us? You mean me as well? But what for?"

"For dancing the morris, my love – England's traditional dance. It starts this morning at eleven thirty."

"You are joking!"

"Fetch me the programme and I'll show you where we'll be ..."

Billy was too dumbfounded to resist. He went to the lounge to fetch the programme. It was like bringing your own death warrant.

"Thank you, love." She flipped over the pages, squinting hard, 'til she found the bit she wanted. "There you are, you see. There's a picture of them, too."

Billy stared at the photo in horror: flowery hats, ribbons, grown men prancing round with hankies. Not only was he forced to be at a ludicrous festival, he had to actually do something ludicrous as well.

51

"Mother, I'm a rugby forward, not a dancer."

This was patently obvious. He was built like the proverbial brick outhouse.

"That doesn't matter a jot, William, and you know it. Didn't that cricketer win Strictly Come Dancing last year? You know, that Darren Gooch."

"Gough."

"Whatever. He was stocky, too."

"Huh. He was paid to do it."

It was also patently obvious Mother was using him as a pawn in her game and would not be put off.

"Terry says he'll lend you some dancing clogs."

"Dancing clogs?"

"To give you some encouragement. You're a size ten, aren't you, William?"

Billy nodded meekly. The picture of a prop forward bedecked in flowers and ribbons loomed in his mind. Chas Threadgold would never speak to him again and neither would the rest of the front row.

"You see, it's all fated. And do you know the weirdest, weirdest thing, William? He's a Taurus! I knew it from the moment I met him. My compatible sign! Well, compatible with my Virgoan side. And he's got Cancer rising! Bit mystical. Bit of a dreamer. People scoff at astrology and there's proof positive."

Billy retreated to his room. Mother swallowed three paracetamol, crawled out of bed and started to organise herself in her spasmodic, disorganised way. All the while she was shouting arrangements through the partition.

He made one last attempt to forestall her.

"Mother, aren't you forgetting? I've just recovered from a car accident."

She ignored him and carried on extolling the virtues of dance, astrology and 'trying new things'.

Billy rolled onto his bed and wrapped the pillow round his ears to block out her voice for a few precious seconds.

The picture-postcard trek down one side of Eskdale and back up the other was becoming seriously tedious. Any attempt that Billy made to dawdle was met with a frown and an appealing stretch of the arms.

The workshop was in the Metropole Hotel Ballroom. As with the concerts at the Football Club, the Rifle Club, the Yacht Club and the Darby and Joan Club, this did not quite conform to Billy's idea of what a folk venue should be. It was a grand, Edwardian building overlooking the western foreshore, a place that epitomised the heyday of the English seaside resort. You could imagine the Prince of Wales staying there in 1904, sipping absinthe by the aspidistra, flirting with the chambermaids, flicking cigar ash into the carved mahogany fireplace ...

Mother skipped up the stairway entrance and flashed her all-week tickets triumphantly at the nearest marshal. She swept into the dancehall every inch the prima donna, scanned round and instantly locked onto the target.

"Wait here a minute, William."

Billy diverted to a row of seats by the wall and tried to make himself invisible. Terry 'head steward' Thwaites was organising his morris men. There was a surprisingly good turnout, mostly females but just enough males to make a fist of it. As Mother was wheedling her way into his orbit, Terry took out a penny whistle and ran his fingers up and down the scale. The group was called to order.

"Gather round in a circle, please! Sit you down if you wish."

A circle quickly formed itself. He stepped into the middle, jutted out his bearded chin and with God-like authority, boomed, "Now then! Be afraid! Be very afraid!" Everyone apart from Billy laughed. "No ... you'll enjoy it, you really will! Once you get through the pain barrier and the blisters. So, if I can get us kicked off ... give 'em the handouts, lads!"

He had a Geordie accent, watered down by college or living farther south. He was shaped like an oversized toby jug, more suited to sumo wrestling than dancing.

"Now, all got one? Good! So you're not feeling around in the dark, a few words of explanation. Terry Thwaites's 'Potted History of the Morris'."

He unravelled a scroll down to the parquet floor – the old wedding speech gag. Everyone laughed, apart from Billy. Then he began to explain in mock-serious tones how England's national dance had come about.

"It might have come from 'moresc' or Moorish dancing and was possibly brought back from the crusades. No one really knows. It was referred to as 'Maurice' in the accounts of Henry VII in 1498: aye,

'Maurice daunce for the purveyance of two shillings!' But it fell out of favour. In fact, it was about the time of Cromwell. The Puritans thought it was downright evil! The 'Devil's dance', no less, and it was banned!"

As Terry droned on, Billy caught the odd phrase ... mentioned in Shakespeare ... revived in Victorian times ... many regional styles ... but was mostly staring out of the window, just as he did at school.

"Verity Sharp, God bless her alder clogs, recently did a piece on *The Culture Show*."

At this, the morris men did a 'wee-uuuh!'

"So we're cool now. We're cultural."

"Wee-uuuh!"

"Yes! It's official. Dance the morris and you'll recreate a little bit of English history! Now then, down to the nitty-gritty. We ... the Whitby Cobblers ..."

The morris men bowed and sang 'TA-RA!' "... are a Cotswold Morris side and that's what you lucky lot will be doing to absolute perfection in no time at all."

The morris men nodded and winked and put their thumbs up. They were obviously primed to support every quip or gesture like little goblin helpers.

"Oh, and by the way, we forgot to mention – you'll be giving a public performance by the end of the week!"

The morris men 'wee-uuuhed' yet again. The volunteers gasped, the gasps subsided into giggles, the giggles into nervous muttering. Billy neither giggled nor muttered. His misery was complete. He could have happily strangled a goblin.

"But we're not that cruel ... no ... it'll be on the final Sunday morning, when it's all quietened down a tad! Note that in your diary. Sunday the twenty-eighth of August! D-Day! That is, dance day."

With that, the morris men spread out amongst the volunteers and corralled them into small groups. Within a few confused minutes, several sides were formed up and marched to the four corners of the room. Terry stayed put in the centre, watching sagely, stroking his beard, nodding and sometimes pointing.

"Now then," he said. "Look around you. Those who have a reasonable level of numeracy will quickly work out you are all in sixes. Why, you might ask? Because the Cotswold Morris consists of teams of six. You should all be there or thereabouts. We'll plug any gaps."

Billy's team looked a sorry sight. There was a lanky, straggly haired ex-roadie in a black Led Zeppelin T-shirt and billowing shorts, two geekish, mousy-haired girls, probably sisters judging by their attire, a happy-clappy student called Ben, who was 'absolutely fascinated' by the folk revival, and a thin-faced, dowdy lady, who looked like a greying Connie Fisher. The instructor, oddly called Ted Morris, got them to stand in line in front of him. He spoke in a monotonous, teacherly drone.

"First of all, I shall endeavour to demonstrate the basic steps you might be called on to use in the dancing of the morris. The step we more commonly deploy in the Cotswold style is as follows … please note the alternate use of the heel and the toe …"

He began plonking one foot heavily in front of the other, like a circus horse doing the counting trick.

"One-two-three, one-two-three! That is the basic step. Of course, the rhythm of the music dictates somewhat, but I shall go more into that later. 'One step at a time', as they say!"

They began to practise while he clapped out the rhythm. Billy immediately shook some change out of his pockets. The others carried on around him while he searched on hands and knees. It was all he had for the day. Eventually, he pocketed a last fifty pence and joined in, keeping the cash tight in his hands. Soon, everyone was skipping in time. Apart from Billy. Ted called them to a halt and pulled him from the middle to the end of the line.

"You'd be better off here, son."

He gave them a two-minute break while he went to consult with Terry in a quiet corner, then strode back purposefully.

"Right. Ready? I want you to follow me round in a complete circle, using that heel-toe step."

He sprang into motion and the line tagged on behind him. Every other group was doing the same thing at the same time. The hall quickly became a tangle of circles clashing into each other. It was like the deck of the Titanic. Billy was already being given a wide berth.

This, he thought, is never going to work. I'll end up killing someone.

On the way round, he noticed Mother had got herself into Terry's group. She was wild-eyed and flushed with excitement. Miraculously, everyone got back to their original spot at roughly the same time.

Terry strode into the centre and bellowed, "That was the easy part.

Now you've got to do the same again ... in a pattern ... to music. Otherwise known as 'dance'. Basic figure, lads!"

On this instruction, Ted arranged the group into two lines of three. Billy was partnered with the Connie Fisher lookalike at the end. She smiled nervously.

"Now then, rude mechanicals," Terry shouted, "we're going to walk you through the basic dance. See how you get on. Just do as your instructor tells you! Ray ... music! Let battle commence!"

And the battle lasted for two hours, by which time Billy's head was spinning. Too much information. Too much skipping. The groups began to break up and drift towards the door, chattering excitedly. Mother had latched onto Terry like a limpet to a shoreline rock. She led him across the dance floor, eager for him to meet her son. Billy's face went to red alert.

"Terry, my son William. William, this is Terry Thwaites."

"Hello there, William. Enjoy it then?"

Billy could only really say yes. The gigantic figure was standing right next to him. A bead of sweat dripped off his bulbous nose onto Billy's trainer.

"Brilliant!"

"See, I said he would. Boys have to be so macho, don't they? All testosterone, no brain. Actually, it's bloody hard work, isn't it?" Terry said, nudging him playfully.

Billy was tempted to nudge him back with interest, but managed to restrain himself.

"William, we're going for a quick half, love, and there's an afternoon concert. It's Green Machine again and Jed Brownlow. Do you want to come?"

The invite wasn't at all convincing.

"Er, no, I'm too shattered ... and the dog ..."

"Yes ... the dog. That's all right then. We'll catch up with you at the caravan."

He set off along the front, past the monument and along Pier Road, where legions of holidaymakers were shuffling along. Candyfloss, seafood, sweets and fish and chips mingled into a vast curry of smells. As he snaked along between tattooed shoulders and buggies laden with bags, someone shouted at him from above.

"Our Billy ... where have you been?"

When Rugby and Morris Meet

Nan and Grandad were coming down the steps of that world-famous fish and chip Mecca, the Magpie Restaurant. He'd forgotten the lunch arrangement altogether.

"Been with Mother dancing ..."

"Oh yes. She told us she'd signed you up for something or other. Never thought she was a dancer. You missed your chips, lad. Delicious ... best in the country they say. Maybe the world."

"Yes, Should have seen the queue! All down these steps and into the road," Nan said, dabbing her lips with a tissue.

"Yes. People come from all over. Stone's throw to the harbour, see. Can't get fresher than that, unless you dive in and pull one out yourself! We'll take you next time." Grandad was rubbing it in. "Anyway, Billy, You don't look like you're starving!"

"Did you enjoy your country dancing?" Nan asked.

"Morris, not country. It was all right."

"Are you going again?"

"Huh. Looks like I've got to. It's on all week and then we have to do a dance in public."

"In public? Our Billy the next Billy Elliot. What a shame we won't be here to see that, John ..." Nan said, genuinely impressed. She'd been something of a dancer herself before she got married.

"Well, we're not coming back special, me duck, so don't you get carried away."

Billy had forgotten they were heading home in the morning. He would have to cope with Mother's affairs alone.

"Could be taking over from your rugby, I reckon!"

Grandad was rubbing his nose in it. Inghams were not known for the performing arts. The last dance he'd done himself was the twist and that was in The Miller's Thumb in the sixties. His stag night.

The mirth faded as they struggled wearily along, dodging the hordes. Being polite country folk, they stepped off the pavement more than their fair share. Grandad was getting flummoxed – he was more at home in a field than a street – but Nan wanted more gifts to take home. She browsed along Sandgate, ogling at the windows full of knick-knacks and jewellery made of Whitby jet. Every now and then, she would disappear inside and then reappear half an hour later with a bag of fudge, a stick of rock or a corny seaside figurine. Although neither of them liked holidays, they had to make other people think they did.

The Whitby Dancer

On the way up Church Street, Grandad winked, took a five-pound note from his wallet and handed it to Billy. They were near the last chip shop before the long climb up to the site.

"As if we'd forget you!"

By the time they arrived, Nan was flagging. The long, slow slog up Green Lane was about as much as she could manage. The quick way up by the 199 steps to the church was beyond her arthritic hips. When they finally arrived at the caravan, utterly exhausted, Grandad sat her down and started blundering around the kitchen, intending to put the kettle on. But he was to catering what Billy was to dancing. She sighed and hauled herself up to make the tea and to find the tomato sauce for Billy.

"A woman's work is never done."

Billy was out on his feet after the surprisingly tough workshop followed by the gigantic seaside portion of chips. But he still felt obliged to take Twiggy for a walk. He always did, even after the hardest match. She lay stretched out on the rough coconut welcome mat with her head between her paws.

"Poor thing. She thinks she's back at the dog rescue," he said, clipping the lead onto her collar. "Left alone for hours. Nothing to do."

Billy slogged up to the Abbey Plain wearily. Twiggy was pulling at the lead until she choked. He let her loose to let off steam while he rested on a rough-made stile. Corn buntings were dipping over a stone wall nearby and hanging off the ears of ripe barley.

When she eventually raced by a fraction too close, he managed to catch hold of her collar. He felt much better now, well enough to take her as far as the lighthouse at Black Nab. It was a hot, windless day and Billy could see miles out to sea. He felt he could almost reach over and touch the passing tankers.

They retraced their steps along the cliff walk and then cut inland beside the Abbey Museum car park. The vast tarmac plain, large symmetrical signs and lines of cars looked out of step in a landscape so dominated by nature. An engine roared and a battered white van with faded lettering on the side drew up by the entrance. It was the same one from the first concert. Someone tumbled out laughing hysterically. It was Mother. Terry heaved himself out of the driver's seat and chased round the bonnet. He pulled her towards him and embraced her in a playful bear hug. She squealed with delight, like an adolescent girl fending off a first kiss. He gave her a peck on the cheek and chased back round to the open door. They laughed uproariously. He revved up and did a three-point turn and she waved as he drove off. He responded with a thumbs-up out of the window. Love makes such fools of people.

"Game, set and match, Twigs," Billy said. "I wonder how long this'll last …"

5

A Handkerchief Too Many

Come Sunday, the grandparents were up early, surreptitiously packing. They had brought so little, it took them no more than a matter of minutes. A prisoner at Guantánamo Bay probably had more stuff than them. Twiggy sat watching in confusion. People putting things in bags meant she might be on the move again.

Billy crept into the lounge area to see them off. Mother was still in bed, gurgling like a drain. Last night, soon after Billy saw the embarrassing romance scene, she had gone back for tea, spent an hour mugging up on Folk and Roots, then was off out again. She took in several concerts, followed by the big Saturday night ceilidh. Grandad said by now she could probably audition for *The Lord of the Dance*.

"There's no need to disturb her, Billy. She's whacked out with all these late dos."

Nan was whispering. She wanted to get away with a minimum of fuss.

"You will be all right, won't you, Billy?"

She was fishing for reassurance. She'd never been apart from him since his move to Brandywell. She had grown close to him, closer than she was to her own son.

"Oh, I'll be OK, Nan. It's only for ... one, two ... five more days," Billy said, shrugging his shoulders.

"It'll go in a flash, love."

"Aye and then there's the grain harvest to look forward to," Grandad said.

Billy pictured himself on the side of the combine, consumed in a whirlwind of dust, heat and engine noise. He could almost feel the bits of husk sticking to the sweat on his brow. It was the hardest of work but it was much preferable to being left in the lurch here.

Grandad picked up the suitcases and stole outside as quietly as his ample frame would allow. He would never make a spy. He opened the

The Whitby Dancer

back of the Land Rover, grimaced and then grinned as it creaked. He loaded up gently while Nan ferried out the small boxes of gifts, snacks and odds and ends that were standing ready in a neat line on the Formica worktop. Billy picked up Twiggy and wedged her under his arm. He tiptoed to the steps to see them off.

"I'll be here round about twelvish on Sunday, lad," Grandad said in a gruff whisper. "Depends how the milking goes. But make sure you're ready for the off."

With that, he tapped Billy's shoulder with a clenched fist and climbed into the car.

Nan took a firm hold of Billy's free hand and squeezed it. Twiggy licked her arm, smothered in liver spots and freckles. In turn, she ruffled the top of Twiggy's head so vigorously she turned her ears inside out.

"And your Sunday lunch will be ready for you the minute you get back!"

She smiled and waved and then struggled up into the high seat not designed for elderly ladies. She wound down the window to mouth some final words, like a lip-reader.

"Promise you'll ring us every day, Billy! Every day at five!"

There was a site telephone not 10 metres from the van, so there was no excuse.

"Course I will, Nan."

"If you don't, we'll be ringing your mother's mobile."

"I'll definitely ring then!"

"Good. Oh, and I've left a note of instructions for her by the cooker."

Grandad let the handbrake off so the Land Rover glided silently down the slope in neutral. A few metres from the site entrance, he turned the ignition key. Nan gave a last wave and an encouraging smile. Billy watched them wind down the lane until they disappeared behind a row of cottages. He put Twiggy down on the top step.

"Wait there, girl ... wait!"

He went inside to get her lead. He wanted to make the most of the last few moments of freedom.

They did the familiar circuit, Twiggy leading the way to her favourite gateposts. When they got back, the silence in the van, the lack of activity, made the atmosphere thoroughly disconcerting. Billy sat down with *Rugby World*, wondering how on earth he would survive the week with nothing to do but prance around for two hours a day.

A Handkerchief Too Many

It was mid morning before Mother stirred. She called out in that limp, pleading way that turned Billy's stomach.

"Oh, William! Come in here a minute, my love, please, please, please … there's something I want to tell you."

In the morning, without make-up, she looked as drained as one of Dracula's victims. She was propped up on her elbow, fumbling around for something on the bedside table.

"I wish he'd never started me off again. Still, we are on holiday. Got to let your hair down sometime!" She was desperate for the tobacco, Rizlas and filter tips that Terry had treated her to. "Listen, love. Something's cropped up. Really, I'm a bit annoyed you didn't wake me up to see them before they set off. Didn't I ask you to?"

"No. I never saw you."

"Well, I'm sure I must have mentioned it. You're getting like your father, William. Only remember what you want."

"You didn't ask me or I would have done it!"

"I'm not going to make a big issue of it. We can phone them later to let them know."

By this time, she had located all the paraphernalia. She painstakingly forged a roll-up with shaking hands and lit up with a flourish. Billy noticed she had a posh Whitby jet lighter. She took one endless drag and stared at the wall. All systems seemed to be crashing.

"Mother. Tell them what?"

"Tell them? Oh. Yes! We're going to stay for an extra week. Yes … 'til Sunday the fourth. That'll be nice, won't it, William? I rang the Carpenters from Terry's last night. They said we could stay as long as we wanted."

"An extra week? That's September! What about Twiggy?"

"What about Twiggy? She loves it here."

"And what about me helping Grandad?"

"Excuse me, but there are laws about child labour. This isn't a Third World country. He'll have to manage for once."

Billy's systems were crashing now.

"The thing is, William, I really need this. Terry's been so kind and he's dancing at Goathland the week after next and at Danby Dale for the National Trust. Local, you see … and he says I could come along to help out, and so could you."

The Whitby Dancer

"I agreed to come for one week! I'm supposed to be ill and I've got stuff to do! It's nearly school for a start."

"William, please! It's for me. For once in my life, I want to do something for 'me'. What's an extra week? It's not as if you're missing anything."

"I'll die of boredom. It's bad enough now, when there's a festival on."

"Huh! I knew I could count on your support."

She flew out of bed. A musty odour wafted across the room as she threw down the cover. She stubbed the cigarette out in a saucer on the narrow dressing table and then stared angrily at the mirror.

"One bloody chance in life I get. A golden opportunity and my own son thinks I'm boring! Boring? Me? Shovelling cow muck into a barrow ... that's boring. Driving round a field all day in a tractor ... that's boring."

"I didn't say you were boring."

"As good as. For the sake of a few days, you'd spoil everything between us."

Billy could see it was hopeless.

"OK! OK! I'll stay another week."

She hugged him melodramatically.

"We will enjoy it, William. You'll see. You'll treasure these special memories with your mother in years to come. I've had such a God-awful time ... If you only knew what I've been through."

He knew all too well. Every gory detail. After a few sniffs and sobs, her mood miraculously changed.

"Now, what time is it? William, why didn't you say? We'll be late for rehearsal."

"Rehearsal on a Sunday?"

"Of course. The show must go on and all that!"

What is it those puritans called it? The 'Devil's Dance'? To Billy Ingham, that's exactly what it became. As the Sunday morning session unfolded, any novelty value quickly disappeared. The task of moulding random shapes and sizes, random ages and levels of competence into teams was proving impossible. Terry had bitten off more than he could chew and he could chew plenty. Before long, he was setting his sights lower, experimenting with a 'molly' dance – a looser, less disciplined type of

A Handkerchief Too Many

morris. "Nil desperadum. They can miss the odd step and no one will notice." He reduced the figures down as much as possible, 'til they were little more than 'primary school stuff'. It was already crisis management.

Billy was quickly labelled 'the oafish one at the end'. He always seemed to be half a beat off the rhythm and 3 metres from where he should have been. Mother watched from the other side of the room, convinced he was trying to sabotage the whole thing. Typical bloody-minded Ingham! she thought.

She seemed to have forgotten he was still on a walking stick only three weeks before. Later, back at the caravan, she made him do an extra rehearsal. Luckily, she was meeting Terry in the Middle Earth at seven for a Scrawny Dog sing around – part of the festival fringe. By the time she had gone, it felt like all the physiotherapy had been undone. Billy collapsed onto his bed and fell asleep within seconds.

On Monday, things got even worse. Terry took Corinne to one side and told her Billy wasn't a natural. Billy could have told him that for nothing. Apparently, he moved like a 'blancmange on a pogo stick'.

"Listen, Corinne, I've had an idea. Did you know that every morris side used to have a fool, why aye! It's perfectly within the tradition. Perhaps we can make up a routine for the lad ... let him float around at the fringes."

Mother pleaded, but for the rest of the session Billy was made to lope around his colleagues like the village idiot. But it wasn't funny. You have to get something right before you can do it entertainingly wrong.

That afternoon, Mother and Billy barely spoke. She retired to her room to catch up on her sleep. Billy did the usual bird watching and sea gazing, but even that was losing its sheen. He felt uneasy all the time, knowing the next session of dance torture was just around the corner. At six, Mother eventually dragged herself out of bed. She got ready untypically quickly, mumbled something about getting himself some chips for tea, and then went off for the usual evening gigs and dances. Billy took the chance to sneak into her room. He left her birthday present at the end of the unkempt bed – he'd bought a Kate Rusby CD in the craft fair at the Pavilion. He wasn't much inclined to get her anything, but the consequences of no card and no gift were too dreadful to contemplate. He spent the rest of the evening trying to watch the prehistoric portable TV, which only got three quivering channels if you were lucky. He fell asleep on the hard lounge seating and didn't hear another thing that night. Neither did Twiggy.

He was woken on Tuesday morning by Mother cheerfully faffing around him. She was in high-energy mode and was about to set off.

"Your dog needs feeding. She's pestering me to death here. Ouch, go down! Don't you dare be late, William ... eleven ..."

She breezed out with no mention of the present. In fact, she said nothing at all about the birthday all through the Tuesday rehearsal! When Billy arrived ten minutes late, the sides were already lined up. Mother ignored him completely. They orbited around each other with hardly a glance. It was becoming embarrassing – she seemed like a stranger. Billy was starting to think he'd got the wrong day or maybe she'd decided to disown him yet again. Not that he was bothered; he just wanted to know the score, so he could ring Nan and get back to Brandywell and normality as soon as possible.

But as soon as the last practice figure spun to a halt, she sauntered over towards him and said, in a matter-of-fact way, "William, I won't be staying at the caravan tonight. Terry's having a late do for me being as it's my birthday. At his cottage. With some friends. Friends you don't know. You don't mind, do you?"

Mind? He could have kissed her.

"Course not!"

"You are a love when you try. We can have our own little celebration another time. Oh, and thank you so much for the CD ... and that card, William! I do prefer the humorous ones." It was a comedy birthday card with a '100' badge and message from the Queen. "And do you know what Terry gave me?"

"No."

"The best present I've ever had. He's writing me a song: *On the Cusp*. It's about us."

"Wow!"

"Yes, fame at last! Clever, isn't it? Because I was born on the cusp and in a way, we're on the cusp, too! On the cusp of something wonderful! Now, are you really, really sure you don't mind?"

"What? About the song?"

"No! Me staying out."

"Mother, just enjoy your party, I'll be fine!"

"I'll see you first thing tomorrow. You're a sensible lad, sensible enough to look after yourself for one night."

On Wednesday, three of the morris men gave up the ghost and stormed out with their bells jangling. Even the most loyal goblin has his limits. They preferred their usual folk-festival routine – a ten-minute performance outside a pub, then several hours inside. Recruits were dropping like flies, too. Every group was so depleted the fool idea was abandoned and Billy was sheepishly drafted back into the side!

"There's no option. We're firefighting now," Terry said quite openly.

The session was extended, then the extension extended. The 'holiday' had become one long morris dance.

Meanwhile, Twiggy was showing signs of clinical depression. When Billy got home, she'd chewed the arm of a fold-up chair into soggy splinters. For the rest of the afternoon, he kept her close by and even took her down to the shops to buy her some chew sticks. By the time he rang Nan, she was still not herself, though she did yap feebly when the old girl shouted, "Poor Twiggy-Twiggy," down the line.

Later, Billy took her for a long, limitless walk and let her run wild in the fields by the cliffs until sundown. She was like a phantom streaking along the drystone walls and disappearing in and out of rabbit holes. Billy got home at ten thirty; there had been no sign of Mother all day.

Thursday the twenty-fifth of August – three days to go to the ordeal and somehow Billy finally got the gist. That is to say, he ended up more or less where he should have been. Typically, Mother and Terry had not turned up to witness his improvement. Someone let it slip they were suffering from 'the mother and father of all hangovers', so Ted Morris ran the session.

He said to Billy, sagely, "You probably got on better today because they weren't there piling on the pressure!"

In truth, Billy was now a fringe event in Mother's new life. For the second time he was being sidelined, while she pursued a 'meaningful relationship'. It had rapidly become the caravan version of *Home Alone*. From the day of her birthday, Mother never stayed at the campsite again. Yet Billy scrupulously rang Nan every day at five and did not spill the beans. As far as she knew, everything was fine. Mother was swanning around somewhere in the background, Twiggy was behaving herself like

The Whitby Dancer

a show dog, the morris dancing was 'brilliant' and Billy was eating properly and sleeping as sound as a bell. None of that was true, of course, but there was an up side – it was Billy's first real taste of living alone with all its blissful freedoms. He could do what he wanted, when he wanted and there was no one here to bother him. The only fly in the ointment was the thought of that Sunday performance: D-Day. It loomed on the horizon like the exam you dread most.

By Friday, the original muster had shrunk to three teams. A much-reduced routine was settled on and the handkerchiefs were finally introduced. It was meant to be a formality, but for Billy Ingham, the simple act of waving something in time to music while dancing was impossible. It sent him right back to square one. Terry was cast into despair. When the session was over, he took Billy to one side and demonstrated the correct method step by step, wave by wave, but with seething, barely controlled anger. Still the lad could not get it. Terry eventually gave up with a sigh, thrust a demo tape of The Whitby Cobblers into Billy's hands and slunk off. Mother ran after him and didn't say goodbye.

The rest of the day was spent in the caravan humming *There Was a Lass on Richmond Hill* and trying to coordinate the foot with the hand. Twiggy bounded up and down trying to snatch the hankies. The van rocked alarmingly. Passing campers glanced at number twenty-three and put two and two together. Every now and then Billy would stop mid-skip and scrum push a wall in sheer frustration.

Saturday came – one day to go. The last rehearsal was passing all too quickly. By now, Terry Thwaites could only stand back and watch his dreams dissolving in the cruel light of day. Billy stumbled around like a bull in a china shop. It had no comic potential. He looked like a bull in a china shop. The remaining morris men, four in all, were too 'hacked off' to bother any more – their attitude being, 'Thwaites has made his own bed, he'll have to lie on it.'

But then something unexpected happened. It was the very last run-through of the very last session. The hotel manager was buzzing round, trying to clear the room ready for a wedding reception. Led Zeppelin, at the end of his tether, grabbed Billy by the arm, swung him round and spoke to him eyeball to eyeball.

"Look, Billy! For God's sake, stop trying to remember things and simply copy the girl in front of you! Monkey see, monkey do!"

"All right! All right!"

The spiky lady opposite nodded her agreement and, as the music started, she helped by pushing him into the correct position. The girl in front, one of the super-efficient sisters, had really 'got into it'. She never put a foot wrong. Billy duplicated her every move a split second behind the beat, but he got through. A little hunched and clumsy, but he got through. Terry was elated. Mother was elated. The hotel manager was elated. Billy was relieved. As he was changing out of the heavy clogs Terry had loaned him 'and wouldn't take no for an answer', Mother skipped over.

"See, I said you could do it! I'm really, really proud of you, William."

"You didn't say that yesterday."

"You didn't deserve it yesterday. You're almost there now! Terry thinks you've got a future. Listen, love, he thinks it's about time he got to know you better. He wants you to come over this afternoon."

"Well, actually, my diary is a bit full, Mother."

"Don't be sarky. It's not becoming for someone of your age."

"That's OK then, because I won't be coming."

Billy could be quite witty sometimes.

"Hmm. I see you've inherited your father's tongue as well as his temper. Here ..." Mother sketched a rough map on the notes page of her diary and tore it out. "It's easy to find, sort of in-between the harbour and the camp. See, if you just take the footpath from the abbey down to The Ropery, then the road that runs above Church Lane, it's down these steps ... really close."

As she pointed, Billy squinted at the scrawl. If it was that close, how come she couldn't be bothered to pop back sometimes? He was tempted to say something but kept his own counsel.

"We'll be back there in an hour, William, so you'll catch us there just after that."

"What about Twiggy?"

"Twiggy! You talk about that creature as if she were human. I'm afraid she'll have to stay in the caravan this evening. We want you to come with us to the Pavilion, you know, the venue on the clifftops where the craft fair is. Perhaps you can slip back to check on her before we go to the final concert there."

The Whitby Dancer

Billy was thrown. He was already consumed with guilt over the dog and certainly hadn't planned on getting chummy with Terry or enduring the final shindig.

When he got back to the caravan, he gave her double the usual mix of Tender Cuts and gravy bones. He had a quick wash and skimmed off the few wispy hairs from his chin and cheeks, before changing into his England rugby shirt as an open act of defiance. He would go in hard, offend everyone, skip the concert and take the dog for an extra-long walk later. He was ready, but not ready. He sat down and started browsing through the *Angling Times* to occupy his mind for a while.

It was mid afternoon before Billy plucked up the courage to go. It was, indeed, only a short way down from the campsite to Terry's. It was in the middle of a row of fishermen's cottages, built on a slope at right angles to the top road. Billy came to the end wall and looked down. He could pick out Terry's white, stuccoed cottage easily. Like all the others, it had the traditional red pantile roof and tiny square windows, but each pane of his glass had a 'Folk Week' flyer fitted into it. Billy wondered how a penniless musician could afford such a place. Terry hadn't been in 'normal' work for years.

"He plays the game on his own terms," Mother had said several times over the week.

Billy carefully negotiated the uneven steps down the slope – one slip could topple you on to the jumble of roofs below. God help the drunks of Whitby, he thought. One false move and they'd end up in the river.

As he got to the last step, he could see the varnished end of a log: Scrawny Dog Cottage. Mother was already at the window with a grin like a Cheshire cat.

Terry opened the door and invited him in with a mock bow.

"Your coat, sir." He looked for humour in every situation. "Come in, Billy. Take a pew!"

Mother was already familiar with kitchens and kettles and music systems. She busied herself like the ideal housewife while Terry played the host. He patted her backside as she passed him. Yes. They were already that familiar.

"It's 'er from there who comes and does," he said, winking.

She was preparing hotdogs and oven chips. He offered Billy a can of John Smith's and Mother accepted on his behalf through the hanging beads that constituted a kitchen door.

"It's all right, William. Just the one!"

Terry opened the can in transit and it frothed onto both of their hands.

"Sit yersel' down, hinny."

Billy sat in a wicker chair and wondered what 'hinny' meant.

"How old are you, hinny?"

"Sixteen"

"Ha! Sixteen. When I was your age, I was an apprentice welder in the shipyard in Newcastle. Course that was when we still made ships in this country."

The history of Terry Thwaites had begun. He was a bright lad, who quickly got bored of welding. He left to join the Merchant Navy and ended up in the Falklands. It was a rough job. He was on deck when an Exocet just whizzed past his ear. When he got back, he happened to pick up Bert Weedon's Play in a Day in a shop in Liverpool. Taught himself on a long trip to Rio ... then the whistle, then the mandolin ... He started his first band in 1987. A Lindisfarne tribute band, Far-ne-way. Scrawny Dog sprang out of nowhere. They were good. They'd been on *Folk Weave.*

"Now there was a show ... much better than that tosser Mike Harding. He's got something against English traditional – he plays anything but that. Usually Irish apart from when it's the Folk Awards and he has no choice then, because some people actually vote for English stuff!"

He went on to explain the new wave that was being discovered by the media, the dance revival, his latest side, his latest instrument, his latest song. Oh yes, Terry Thwaites wrote his own material, too. As Mother came in with a platter full of steaming hotdogs, Terry broke into *The Sinking of the Gaul* with a gravelly, guttural voice that propelled beer fumes across the room. About 300 verses later, he finished. The dogs were no longer hot.

"Yeah. True story: a Hull trawler that sank in mysterious circumstances. They reckon it was a spy ship and the Russians sank it. Course, the government denied it, wor Billy ..."

'Wor Billy'? Where did that come from? Billy wondered.

Terry proceeded to retell in words what he had just sung about. For the next three hours, he held court. Mother sat adoringly at his knee, hanging on every word as if he were some sort of guru. Billy nodded and smiled, but was somewhere on a rugby field in the Midlands. As Terry was about to start another yarn, Mother sprang to her feet.

"Terry! I've just realised! It's nearly eight!"

"Ha! The little lady wants to dance!" Terry said patronisingly.

He lumbered upstairs to change into a fresh official T-shirt. Billy wallowed in the silence.

They made their way along the harbour, over the swing bridge and up the steps to the North Promenade. From just past the Cook Monument they could see the Metropole Hotel in the distance – the thought of that rehearsal room turned Billy cold. He was starting to despise the place. As they approached the Pavilion, which was built below the level of the promenade and jutted out over the beach, a wild sea thrashed against the sea walls and rain was on the wind.

Terry led the way down the steps to the venue. He suddenly stopped and cocked an ear. "That's them, har-har! The Lords of Misrule – I can hear 'em – one of the best dance bands in the country," he said. "I taught them everything they know!"

They were nodded into the dance hall and as soon as the caller announced the next dance, Terry whisked Mother onto the floor. Mother looked back towards Billy, who was left stranded on the margins. She pointed towards a group of girls standing expectantly nearby. Billy was having none of it. Being made to learn the morris was one thing, but this was the open market. Mother, Terry, a caller, a bunch of wild horses could not make him ask a girl for a dance. And even in the folk world girls don't ask unprepossessing boys. He accepted his fate and shrank into himself like a snail into its shell.

He endured it as long as he could, then, between a reel and a polka, he chicaned round the rows of dancers to catch up with Mother. She was as high as a toddler at Christmas.

"Going? You haven't given it a chance, have you?"

"But I've got to see to the dog! And I'm totally shattered!"

"How can you be? You just sat there."

"You should try smashing your head on the road some time."

A timely accordion struck up and she was pulled away again. Billy didn't catch her reply.

He fled through the mad whirl of dancers and out of the hall. He climbed back up the same spiral staircase they'd come down not an hour before. High above the raging shoreline, he walked furtively on as

A Handkerchief Too Many

if escaping the scene of a crime. As the music faded, the wash of the sea took over. Perhaps Mother was right – he should have given it a chance. There were plenty of girls and only a handful of lads. It was a golden opportunity to face up to his crippling shyness and he had blown it.

When he got back, the storm had grown so angry the caravan was bobbling about on its axles. Twiggy was too spooked to make a fuss of him; she just whimpered and nuzzled his shins. He made a mug of tea, handed her a succession of biscuits and rolled onto his bunk bed. She settled at his feet. Only sleep could rescue him from the miserable situation. The dog would have to do without her walk for once.

At nine thirty he was woken by a fierce hammering on the bedroom window. It was Mother.

"William! Are you up? We need to get going. Terry's got so much to do!"

Billy unlatched the door. Twiggy sprang up and nipped at Mother's sleeve.

"William, this is my best top! Please put that dreadful animal in the bedroom."

"But she can come with us! I'm not leaving her all by herself for another day!"

Yesterday was the last straw. He would take her along or pull out altogether.

"For heaven's sake! What will you do with her while you're dancing?"

"If she doesn't go, neither do I! There's plenty of seats to tie her to. Other people do it."

"William, it's a serious demonstration. I'm sure you can do without the dog for a solitary hour."

But Billy dug his heels in.

"She's getting really strange ... she's not herself ... if Nan found out ..."

Mother caved in, but only because there would be no one to take Billy's place.

"You'd better make damned sure she's properly tied up. We don't want her spoiling the performance. Terry's put body and soul into this."

Mother stood at his shoulder as he got ready and harried him along. She scanned around for suitable things to wear and her eye alighted on a pile of fresh clothes. At the top was a clean T-shirt.

The Whitby Dancer

"That'll do, William! Quickly."

She didn't know it had a 'Shirlington High U-16's Orcs on Tour' motif on the back.

Billy hated these high-octane episodes that Mother sprang on him. He was still gnawing away at a piece of dry crust as they raced down the site road into the morning mist. All around them Billy noticed that many folkies were already packing up and heading for home. There was a downbeat, end-of-term feel in the atmosphere.

Terry was standing sentinel at the Metropole door, ticking names off as the dancers arrived.

"Hi, Terry!" Mother said, pecking him on the cheek. "How's it looking?"

"Good stuff, Coz," he replied. "In fact, very good stuff. Reckon they've all turned up! Wonders never ... and we've got time for a last run through before we face the music. Oh! Did you have to bring the mutt?"

Mother cast a sideways look at Billy and frowned.

"Er ... sorry ..."

Without asking, Terry grabbed the lead off Billy and the dog was dragged away from him. She skidded and scrambled on the parquet floor, until she was handed over to a portly, breathless lady of middling years at the side of the room. It was Heidi Smart – one of Terry's long-standing entourage. Heidi usually fussed round Terry as much as Mother did. Mother had been suspicious of her at first, but Terry reassured her that Heidi was 'history'. Heidi, however, thought she was still current affairs. She scowled and retreated to the farthest corner, dragging the mutt behind her. She was always willing to help Terry Thwaites, but dog-sitting at short notice was the ultimate test of her devotion.

Ted Morris was busy sorting out and lining up the three surviving teams. When the melee was sufficiently settled down, Terry stepped forwards.

"Now then. We'll give each of you a spin. Don't worry what happens in here. Better you make the mistakes now rather than later. Get 'em out of your system. Leave 'em at the door. You did well yesterday; just relax and think of England! So, first, the whippersnappers ..."

The team of youngest dancers formed up excitedly. They were draped in makeshift ribbons and hats. Ray 'fingers' Cunliffe struck up a chord on the squeeze box and the leader led them off. They had all the zest and confidence of youth and flew through their routine with ease. As the last figure was complete, everyone else broke into spontaneous applause. All the females 'Aah'd'. Terry smirked and rounded them up into a group hug.

"Absolutely magic. Wunderful! The kids have set the bar high! Match that, side number two."

The second team was Mother's. Although a raggle-taggle mix of age, sex and size, they quickly snapped into position. They all wore white tops with black sashes, donated by the regular morris men, that made them look the part. Mother stood out, poised like a heron about to strike.

Ray hammered the first chord before they had time to get nervous. It worked. They did the whole thing with hardly a foot put wrong. Terry strutted around patting himself on the back.

"I guess two out of three's not bad."

He grinned a wide, nicotine-stained grin. Mother ran over to hug him. All this sweetness and light made Billy even more jumpy.

Heidi looked on with distaste. She felt used. Time was she was Terry's right-hand man. Has it come to this? she thought. Who is that dreadful woman? Obviously neurotic. Twiggy was struggling to get off her lead, so Heidi half-throttled her back to heel.

Billy's side was forming up haphazardly. Only the sisters had made any attempt at costume. The student wore a dingy white polo shirt and was sweating profusely from the armpits. Led Zep, as he was now called, was dressed in the usual seventies T-shirt. Connie Fisher had the look of someone just out of electric shock treatment and Billy? Billy had all the elan of a brickie's mate. This time, Ray set off with a much slower tempo and a no-frills Cotswold Morris stuttered into action. They had none of the zest and confidence of youth. Billy was virtually passed around like a very large dummy. Terry watched in horror, gradually twisting his shaggy beard into one thick strand.

"I thought we ditched the slapstick routine, Ray," he said sardonically as the last figure ground to a halt. "And I'm doing gigs for the National Trust next week!"

The team stared accusingly at Billy. Billy thought it had gone quite well.

"Ah well, it'll have to do!" Terry called the sides to order a final time and lined them up near to the entrance. "Don't forget, a disciplined entrance catches the attention. We shall march two abreast to the beat of the drum. Remember, make a noise and get 'em early!"

They jostled into two-by-two order, got the last bits of silliness out of their systems and paraded through the vestibule, down the main steps of the Metropole and into the harsh reality of the outside world. The morris men marshalled them from the sides, while passers-by parted on the pavement. They processed along the North Promenade self-consciously and with none of the usual banter. They came at last to the performance area, the small plaza around the Captain Cook Monument. Here, Terry led them round in a complete circle to announce their presence visually. Billy could see by the smiles and comments they were well and truly noticed. That done, they milled round the monument and waited nervously. A regular morris side, eight men and a fool from Derbyshire, was in mid-performance. It was their last official spot of the festival. A three-deep crowd had gathered to watch them.

They ended their week's work with an extra strong clash of sticks. They turned and marched off wearily, triumphantly, to a welter of applause. There was a feeling of finality in the air.

The crowd fell silent and was starting to disperse, when Terry stepped forwards and boomed, "Thanks, lads, let's hear it once more for High Peak Morris! Good stuff!"

The audience felt obliged to applaud. But before they'd finished Terry boomed again.

"Now then, ladies and gentlemen, waifs and strays, before you depart ... we are The Whitby Cobblers Morris! Over the last few days we've taken up a challenge. Is it possible to train up a side from scratch, and I mean scratch, in a week? I say 'Oh no it isn't!'"

With a sweep of the arms he invited the audience to reply, "Oh yes it is!"

They shouted willingly. With that, their attention had been won back entirely. After several 'Oh Yes/Oh Noes', Terry stroked his beard portentously and declared, "I think it's about time we put it to the test, don't you? Bring on our brand new side ... er ... Whippersnapper's Molly. Give them a round of applause. They've been working really hard. In fact, if you look closely, you'll see they have no backsides, because they've worked their backsides off. Ha! Ha!"

The junior team stepped forwards and all the females 'aah'd. They took up their positions and, as the young do, they assumed that frown of strict concentration. Ray's squeeze box played a long chord to set them up and the fiddler began to play. They snapped into motion as one. The rustling of clothes, the tapping of steps added to the spectacle. The crowd swelled. Billy cast his eye around to see where Heidi was. She was perched on the end of a corporation seat leaning on the arm. An old lady to her side was being overwhelmed by her bulk. Twiggy was crouching at her feet and looked tiny in comparison to her. Every now and then, she caught a glimpse of her master and tugged impatiently. Heidi tugged her violently back. She preferred cats. Especially today.

The youngsters finished bang on the beat with a flourish. A tumultuous round of applause echoed off the hotel frontages nearby. They looped off, still in twos, smiling and flushed with success. They only broke rank when Terry nodded his approval. The applause petered out and Terry, with an encompassing sweep of the arm, signalled to Billy's team to get ready. He'd decided to send them on next. It was an old trick – hide the worst in the middle. Billy's nerves were jangling. Despite the dry August wind blowing off the moors, a trickle of sweat rolled down the nape of his neck. He mopped it with a morris hanky.

Terry strode into the arena.

"Next up, we have a fine body of men. Well, maybe not fine, maybe not men. Same as those, just one week's training ... please welcome the Cobblers Load Morris!"

Those in the crowd who got the joke laughed. Before he knew it, Billy was pushed into position from behind. There was a hush. Ray was poised ready to press the first chord. And in that strange split second, the panic went ... training took over ... the music began ... his right foot automatically stepped forwards on the up beat. Step in, step back, turn right, around to the other end, step in, step back ... all in perfect time with the clompety-clomp, clompety-clomp rhythm of clogs. Terry had said the feet would dance by themselves – muscle memory – and they did!

I'm dancing ... I'm dancing ... he thought.

The first whirling of the hankies came ... he did it ... the diagonal weaving ... he did that, too ... all straightforward ... all so bloody easy ... what was all that fuss about? Then, back to the beginning ... off we go again. Step in, step out ... and something even stranger was happening. He was enjoying it. Yes, Billy Ingham, prop forward, two left feet, was actually enjoying the music, the pattern of movement, the harmony of the couplings, the rhythms, the stepping. He was relishing the light, disciplined footfall. Handkerchiefs? They just seemed to wave themselves! It was heady, exhilarating ... it was dance! An absurd thought followed: bloody good rugby training this! Sod Threadgold!

He skipped effortlessly round to his second position, into the middle of the three pairs. Now he was directly facing Heidi.

At that very moment, he saw a striking, light-haired girl, almost albino, bending down to stroke the dog. His concentration collapsed. He didn't weave around the back of his partner as he should have done. Instead, he swerved in front. This made her clash with the sister to her side. It was a disaster. The sister scowled. The other one hissed, "Get yourself behind us!" Connie Fisher waved her arms like a traffic cop. Terry instantly assessed the situation. In the guise of the fool, he joined in the melee and took hold of Billy's arm. By doing the 'Gay Gordons', he dragooned him back into the right slipstream. He spun out to the margin, bantering about 'bloody amateurs' as he went. But the damage was done. The team tried to reboot for the third figure, but it was too late. Within a few bedraggled steps, the six broke ranks completely and Ray broke into the Laurel and Hardy theme tune to make light of the matter. The crowd seemed to enjoy it.

Terry shrugged his shoulders and stepped into the breech. He was going to start them off again. But something else had caught Billy's attention. A tall, gaunt man with a zapata moustache appeared out of the crowd. He was manhandling the girl away. Twiggy was yapping and trying to get after him. Heidi was reeling her in severely. Billy ran over.

"Is this dog of yours trained at all?"

"Excuse me, Mrs Smart ... er ... who was that?"

"Look. They're waiting for you!"

"Yes. I'll be there in a sec. Please, who were they?"

"Oh! She was a foreign girl. For God's sake, calm it down! They're waiting!"

"Is she something to do with the festival?"

"Huh. I think not. An illegal. Too many of them coming in."

Heidi's liberal lifestyle did not extend to 'illegals'.

"But that man ... did he say anything?"

"What man?"

Heidi was so absorbed in Terry's moment of glory and her own personal hell, she didn't notice a girl being abducted.

A Handkerchief Too Many

Meanwhile, Terry was doing some stand-up whilst sorting out the mess. He was about to announce 'Cobbler's Load take two' when he saw where Billy was. He nodded to Mother, trying to get her to get him. Billy, meanwhile, was undoing the loose knot that attached the dog to the arm.

"What the hell are you doing?" Heidi shouted.

She was sitting solidly on part of it. Billy tugged it forcefully from under her and it burned the soft slab of flesh behind her knee.

"Ouch! Do you mind?"

Mother was making her way round the circle, trying not to look flustered.

As Billy stooped to gather up the lead, he noticed a handkerchief draped over Heidi's elephantine foot. It was smudged with make-up and embroidered in one corner with an eagle, the sort of craftsmanship that transfixes the eye.

He looked at Heidi apologetically and said, "Very sorry about that. Here, you've dropped this ..."

"That's not mine!"

He peered at the waiting morris team. They stood poised with hankies at the ready – no one seemed to be missing one. He checked his pockets – his own were still there, stuffed untidily. He pictured the girl in distress, wiping her eyes. What if it was hers? It had to be! Just then, Mother arrived, grabbed his arm pincer-sharp and spoke through gritted teeth.

"You get over there right now and give it another try. Please do not embarrass me further!"

Before she had the chance to say anything else, Billy cupped his hand over his mouth and scurried off with Twiggy at his side. He ran to the edge of the Crazy Golf course 30 metres distant. There, he bent up double and pretended to be sick. He waved at Mother pathetically and then placed his hand on his forehead like a ham actor. Step by step, he was edging further away. By the time he got to the flower beds in The Crescent, the giant frame of Terry was skipping up and down. He had taken his place. Mother had shrunk behind the Captain Cook Monument.

Now, Billy was a big fan of Crufts. Many an evening at Brandywell they had settled down to watch it. He was particularly fond of the search exercise, where a scented cloth is wrapped round a dog's nose and then

The Whitby Dancer

hidden on the other side of the arena. The dog is then dispatched to find it. Twiggy was a wilful, harum-scarum type of creature, a rescue dog that had never been disciplined, never been properly trained or worked. Grandad said he could make a better dog out of pipe cleaners. But Billy had discovered that she was the keenest of hunters, far keener than the gun dogs that Grandad kept.

"It's a long shot, girl … but what else can we do?"

6

Follow Your Nose

Dogs: finely evolved machines, animals that experience the world mostly through their noses. That's how they survived in the wild, the raw, unforgiving desert, the frozen mountainside. Man: he saw the dogs work, saw their efficiency and followed them to food and shelter. It dawned on him he could harness this ability. He tracked them, trapped them, studied them, trained them. They were the most cooperative of creatures, the most malleable. Generations of partnership followed. Where the cave, the pit, the tumulus or the grave give up human bones, they give up dog bones, too. Over aeons, useless factors were bred out and useful ones bred in. Man, dog, became reflections of each other, symbiotic like tree and ivy. In the steppe, the marsh, the jungle, the steepest hill, the deepest ravine, man had gained a crucial advantage, a radar that detected the tiniest hint of prey and homed directly in. Dogs: perfect form, perfect function.

And then came Twiggy. Sure, she had been born into pedigree stock – a fusion of Dalmatian, whippet, bull terrier, pointer ... a mix that was brave, fast, highly prized by the huntsman. But Twiggy Lobelia Cromarty Girl was a tad too long in the leg, they said, a tad too short in the back. No rosettes for her. No good for breeding. So she was dumped, forgotten, until an aimless lad in need of company got her from Shirlington Dog Rescue for the cost of spaying and delousing. Everything about her was wrong. Grandad said so and he knew dogs. Even her nose, long in the breed, was too long in her; freakishly long. But a long nose means more nerve endings, more sensors to take in the millionth part of the faintest scent. In the three short years Billy had owned her, Twiggy had shown herself to be the absolute mistress of the hunt. Physically a joke, practically a clown, but when the quarry was near, she was like a smart missile.

The Whitby Dancer

In exactly the same way tweedy ladies from the shires prepare their charges for the Crufts challenge, Billy wrapped the handkerchief round the end of Twiggy's nose. She snorted it in like some kind of addict. Soon, they were pelting along the Royal Crescent, past the posh bed and breakfasts, down the Avenue, away from the front. The squawking gulls fell silent. She right-angled into a side street, then down a staith, an ancient wharf lane, deep into the oldest part of town. She turned once more into a narrow, poor man's terrace. She stopped in her tracks at the very end. This was it – a salt spray battered cottage. A piece of cardboard had been sellotaped to the corner of the front window: Holiday Home ... ring ... The numbers had been scored out. Sixties pebble-dash was peeling off the side wall. Rose bay and dandelions, sure signs of neglect, pushed up through cracks in the concrete flags.

Billy thought for a second and then prised the rickety front gate open. It squealed on rusty hinges. He picked the dog up, tiptoed up to the window and peeped in, squinting against the reflections. He could see piles of boxes and telephone directories. Old newspapers were scattered on the floor for a makeshift carpet. A door was flung open and a tall, sinister-looking figure hurried into the room; a Dracula of a man with a distinct widow's peak. He stooped over and rifled though a pile of directories. He seemed agitated. He turned sharply and headed for the door. Billy placed his hand round Twiggy's snout and dodged to the side of the house. He just managed to duck behind a large black wheelie bin, when the man sped out and slammed the door behind him. Billy caught a whiff of a very strong aftershave. Heavy footsteps clicked along the stone sets into the distance. He put Twiggy down and crept to the front door. He lifted the lion's head knocker and tapped gently. There was no reply. He tried again, this time rapping with more force. Instinctively, he looked up. She was there! The fair-haired girl was at the window looking down.

She disappeared. Billy heard her coming downstairs. The door was opened, until he could just see her face.

"Yes?"

"Oh, hello. I'm one of the dancers ..."

He pointed at his T-shirt.

Before he could finish, she opened the door fully and knelt to make a fuss of Twiggy. Twiggy responded with licks and whimpers as if she knew the girl already.

Follow Your Nose

"The little dog from the dancing ... we make friends. You are just like my Kaji."

A couple of things were immediately obvious – she was not English and she was kind by nature.

"Yes, I saw you stroking her."

"I think it is my dog come to see me! It make me very sad. She is yours ...?"

"Yes. She goes with me everywhere."

"But what are you doing here? Uncle Luan will be angry ..."

"Luan?"

Billy knew exactly who she meant. She stood up and looked anxiously along the terrace.

"He will be back soon ... you must go. He say I talk to no one in this place."

She edged back inside and started to close the door.

"But I have something for you. I think you dropped this. We followed you, so you could have it back."

He took the fine silk handkerchief from his pocket and handed it to her.

"Oh! It was Mama's. She make in bad times. You are very kind. But how you follow me?" Billy glanced down at the dog. "Ah yes. *Faleminderit!* I mean, thank you. But now you must leave. Luan does not let me speak to anyone." She bent down to give Twiggy a last pat on the head. "I wish you were my Kaji."

Billy saw a chance.

"Listen, I'll be taking her for a walk later. Would you like to come along? It's amazing how she's taken to you. She never does that with strangers. You can meet some of the dancers, too. I know you've been watching us."

"I'm sorry ... I cannot ... not today. Luan does not let me have friends here."

Billy's eyes betrayed his disappointment.

"OK. It was just a thought."

He turned to go. He could almost feel her eyes searing into his back.

"Are you really dancer ... folk dancer?"

'Orcs on Tour' had done the trick.

"Oh, yes. I'm a morris dancer. It's England's traditional dance, you know. Goes back to the Dark Ages. Queen Victoria Cromwell ... very old."

"Morries? I have not heard ..."

"Cobbler's Load ... best in the area ... won prizes ... doing Goathland next week."

"Not possible today. Tomorrow it is Monday. I take washing tomorrow. Yes. He say I must do that for him. There is, what do you say it ... launderette on corner. You see?" She twisted her head and pointed. "I like see you. I will be there at ten. He make me wash everything. Plenty clothes ..."

With that, she closed the door. Billy listened to her footsteps drumming up the carpetless staircase. He looked up at the window a final time and then walked up to the top road to check out if there really was a launderette. There was. He could smell it before he could see it.

He spent the rest of the day bewildered. He couldn't believe what he'd done. He rang Nan at five and simply reeled off the usual assurances. No mention of the morris debacle, dropped handkerchiefs, scent trails or new family rifts. No, just a normal day like all the others.

"No, Mother can't come to the phone just now. She's out buying a Chinese for tea."

What started as little white lies were becoming dingier by the day. But it didn't seem to matter.

Billy had never been on a date before; never had the chance or the bottle. But was this really a date anyway? In a launderette? And would she turn up? For the rest of that evening he was tortured by doubt. Until now, life had not been complicated by the female. His dog came first, then rugby, then the farm. The girls at Shirlington High had no truck with a shy lad, who had neither the pushy edge nor the boy-band looks they required. By his appearance, you could pretty well gauge his nature – solid, unimaginative, unflashy. He would never dream of chatting up thin girls, who talked like the cast of *Friends*, who texted as they walked and who read *Heat* religiously. They seemed to exist in a parallel world, full of celebrities and no sport. Yet, here he was, fascinated by the most exotic-looking thing he'd ever seen, asking to meet her against all his instinct, putting himself through hell on a hunch. At least Twiggy was happy. That evening, she had more walks and more attention than ever. He barely thought about Mother or the inevitable consequences. Perhaps she would never forgive him.

Follow Your Nose

The next morning, after much soul searching, Billy set off without the dog. Monday the twenty-ninth of August was a bank holiday, a fact that had escaped him. The folk scene had moved on, but now the streets were even more chaotic than during the festival. Kids with candyfloss, hordes of day-trippers, bikers with bags of chips – it was impossible to get along comfortably. By now, he knew his way across town like the back of his hand, but only just made it to the launderette in time. He peered through the plate-glass window to check if it was open. It was. A mountainous service wash was stacked by a machine, but the girl was not there. He stood around outside, trying not to look suspicious, pretending to be browsing a rack of postcards outside the gift shop down the way. At precisely ten, he saw her coming around the corner, struggling with a canvas laundry bag on her shoulder and a carrier bag in her hand. He raced along to offer help.

"Hi! Wanna hand?"

"No! No! In my country, women do all work!" she said, smiling.

He wasn't sure if she was joking. He held the door open for her. She squeezed past him sideways and offloaded the bags onto a row of tacky red plastic seats. She opened the door of the nearest machine and quickly transferred everything into it. She slammed the door shut then searched in her pockets for a coin to put in the powder dispenser.

"Two pounds. That is much!"

A small, brightly coloured box clunked down heavily. She ripped the end off, tipped it into the powder tray and then put her remaining coins in the machine – all at neurotic speed.

"I am very sorry yesterday. You were kind to bring my handkerchief and if I was at home, you would have been invited in ..."

In-between her polite smiles there was an air of deep sadness. She fell silent as the wash sequence began. Billy felt he had to say something.

"Are you on holiday?"

"No ... my name is Sofia ... Sofia Zander ... I am from Albania."

"Oh. Have you come for a job?"

"Yes. I am going to be translator for my uncle's company. My uncle is very kind. He is trying to help my family. He is importer. Things are not so good in my country."

"Albania, you say." Billy had never heard of the place.

"Yes. It is near to Greece, and ... er ... Italia." She drew a map in the air with her index finger. "What is your name?"

The Whitby Dancer

"William ... well, Billy, they call me."

"Billy! And where is your little dog, Billy? She was very nice."

"I didn't think I could bring her in here."

"In Albania no problem. Look. I have photo of Kaji."

She took a tiny, laminated photo from her top pocket and handed it to Billy.

"Wow! I didn't know they had English fox terriers abroad."

It was the mirror image of Twiggy.

"It make me happy to see her. I think I am dreaming. I have no friends here. He will not let me go out much, only for this and shop." A look of disgust fell over her face. "I have been here over one week and this all I do."

"I thought he was your uncle."

"He is. And that is why I come here. And that is why my friend Maria come here, too, five weeks ago. He is helping us." Tears welled up in her eyes. "He will not let me ring her. I do not know what is happening. He keep saying there is problem with papers ... Insurance Nationale, but he is doing his best. He is helping us and everything will be all right. When I come I think I am with Maria. He just say I will see her soon and he laugh. Then Mehmet say we will be working in same office very soon."

"It all takes time to get sorted. You haven't been here long, after all."

"I suppose you are right. I need time to practise my English."

There was a long silence as they both thought things through.

"Funnily enough, I think I saw you up on the cliff the other Friday. Very late it was ... about midnight! You know, near the abbey?"

He pointed in the direction of the cliffs.

"Ah, yes! That was me. I do not like house. I try to find hostel. Youth hostel. I see on map. He follow me and say it is dangerous and we have to be careful. He say papers were nearly through. He say I have to stay with him and Mehmet. I do not like Mehmet ... he look at me ..." She began to sob again. "He was rough with me ... I was frightened. He take my passport, my money. I am like prisoner."

Billy didn't know how to react, whether to reassure her, put his arm around her or just jolly things along. Something was deeply amiss. She took a deep breath, stopped up the crying and regained her composure.

"We were in a folk group in Albania. Maria and me. She play gujde. I play clarinet. And I am dancer like you ..."

She stood up sharply, skipped and pirouetted. All of a sudden, folky things took on a whole new meaning.

"I like to see dance. You make traditional dance very good."

Fortunately, she was hauled off before he wrecked the performance.

"Yes. I love morris dancing. That is why I'm a bit sad, too. The festival is over."

"Oh?"

"Yes. It finished on Sunday with the very dance you saw. Pity you didn't stay until the end. I did a bit on my own ... a solo. I don't live in Whitby, I'm afraid. I live in the Midlands. A long way from here."

"Oh! You go soon?"

"Next weekend. I have a week's holiday and then my grandfather's coming to pick me up."

"I wish I was going home. Ah well, Billy. We can be friends for this one week."

Sadness overtook her again. The soapy smell pervaded the atmosphere. The rhythmic slush-slush-slush of the machine drowned out any more conversation. Two elderly ladies came in and cast suspicious looks at the ill-matched couple. Sofia kept glancing at her watch nervously. Billy started to wonder why he had bothered to turn up. He didn't know that first dates are mostly made up of awkward silences. History would record that Billy Ingham's lasted only as long as a hot wash and spin-dry.

As Sofia was emptying the last load, she said without looking at him, "Tomorrow, Billy ... I go shopping. I have to buy food. We have no fridge. We have nothing in house. I will do very quickly. We can meet."

"Yes! Great! Where?"

"The statue where you dance. I tell you more. I tell you what happen."

"What time?"

"Eleven. If I am late, not worry. You will bring Tiggy?"

"Twiggy," he corrected her, though 'Tiggy', if anything, was an improvement.

She folded then pressed a last seventies-style shirt into the carrier, at which Billy opened the door wide, let her through and made to follow in the same direction.

"No, please ... not with me ... he come this way ... he is always nearby ..."

The Whitby Dancer

She hurried along the street, turning once to wave discreetly with her free hand.

Billy made his way home in a fog, completely oblivious to anything around him. At least she would see him again. At least he would have something to do to kill the time. He was fascinated by the unworldly girl with piercing blue eyes but, at the same time, he was uneasy. What was he getting himself into? He had been warned against any more adventures after what had happened the year before. Perhaps he should drop the whole thing. Perhaps he should 'stand her up'. The other lads from school did it as a matter of pride.

Things were getting complicated. Mother had arranged some days ago for him to spend the bank holiday afternoon at Terry's. It took some steeling of the nerves to make himself set off to Scrawny Dog Cottage. Terry answered the door, grunted and turned away. Mother gesticulated for him to sit down.

"And what was that all about?"

"What?"

"The dying swan act."

"I was genuinely sick. Honest."

"And I am genuinely sick of you, William. How come you started off OK, managed the first bit OK, managed the hard bit OK, then suddenly marched off? You didn't look sick to me. You looked positively healthy!"

"Must have been the motion, you know, the spinning round made me dizzy."

"Huh! We took all the spinning round out of it," Terry said.

He was still annoyed. Billy stuck to his story.

"I'm really, really sorry ... I was heaving up all night, too, and I've only just started to feel better." He kept on insisting it was something to do with the accident. "It felt like the concussion was coming back."

After an hour of gushing contrition, he blurted out, "I mean you've got me all wrong – I'd really like to get into morris as a proper hobby."

Perhaps that was not altogether an invention. Sofia had made the idea seem far more attractive.

"Are you being serious?" Mother asked with a look of disbelief.

"Deadly ... I loved it."

The atmosphere lightened and Terry offered him a can of Guinness; yes, Guinness, supercool from an hour in the freezer.

Follow Your Nose

"That'll settle your stomach, lad."

Mother approved with a forced grin. Terry was flattered that he had actually enthused someone.

"Ah well, hinny ... I didn't really mind stepping in at the last moment. It was bound to happen somewhere along the line. Perhaps I was too ambitious."

He offered to show Billy around the house. It was time to introduce him to the mystic ways of folk culture.

"Brilliant!" Billy said.

"We'll take it from the top. Follow me ..."

Terry led him into the narrow hallway. There was a gallery of photos going up the staircase wall. As they went up, he stopped beside each one and pointed.

"Me and the lads at Beverley, me and the lads at Otley, me and the lads at Fylde ..."

'Me and the lads' had been everywhere. Billy noticed Terry always looked exactly the same even twenty years ago. He showed him into the spare room where guitars, mandolins, banjos, bongo drums and hurdy-gurdies stood on stands or hung from walls. Every folk instrument in existence seemed to be there, awaiting his golden touch.

"Yes. Had a band of my own ... Scrawny Dog."

"You told me last time."

"Or The Dogs as we came to be known."

"Er ... I remember you saying."

Terry led him along the landing and past the one dedicated bedroom. The door was ajar – Billy noticed Mother's designer bag draped over the end of a pine double bed.

"This is the archive room. Odds and sods to the uninitiated."

He sat him down at a computer, cleared a space by the keyboard and proceeded to work his way through a mountain of photo albums, press cuttings, scrapbooks and festival programmes, each with a rambling anecdote attached.

"Yeah. That was me and The Incredible String Band at Sherbourne. I got them to re-form ..."

After almost an hour, they finally returned to the living room to listen to scratchy studio recordings of Scrawny Dog. No one has ever devised a better form of torture. Billy distractedly downed several cans of Guinness as the night dragged on and Terry droned on. The false

The Whitby Dancer

smile became painful after about half an hour, but somehow he kept up the act. By the time he stepped out into the cool night air, Billy felt exactly like he did after the accident.

"I'll tak wor Billy doon to see ma bo-at tomorrow!" Terry said to Mother as he staggered off. He seemed to get more Geordie as the drink sank home.

Billy was sick, dizzy and bored out of his mind – but he had rescued the situation.

He took the longest route home. The roar of the North Sea thrashing against the harbour wall seemed to be thrashing against his head. Just two visits and he had got to know the world of Terry Thwaites very, very well. Terry Thwaites, however, had learned next to nothing about Billy Ingham.

Mother slept soundly that night. Terry was so wise, so forgiving. She loved him even more! What a man! Not a grudging bone in his body. And Billy had shown a real interest in something for a change. Things could work out well. Yes ... Taurus, Virgo, Capricorn ... all the earth signs connecting in a sort of cosmic morris. Billy, however, did not sleep soundly. He was plagued by the sort of nightmare you try to wake up from, but you keep nodding off and it keeps coming back. Welcome to the world of alcohol.

In the morning, it took twice as long to get the dog fed and ready. There was no time for vanity. A cold wash and fresh polo shirt would have to do. He was in unknown territory – hangover followed by date.

When he arrived at the monument, Sofia was already there peering from behind the plinth. She had a shoulder bag at her feet, full to the zip-up top with shopping. She seemed more interested in the dog again.

"Tiggy, Tiggy, Tiggy ... I knew you would come." At last, she turned to Billy. "Do you have money?"

Billy was taken aback by her brazenness.

"Yes. I've just been to the wall bank."

"Wall bank? Ah, yes. We can walk on beach down there, then we get coffee. He give me just enough for shopping. I have to give him ... these ... every little one!"

She took some tabs out of the top pocket of her dated, East European blouson and showed them to him.

Follow Your Nose

"Receipts," Billy said.

"Yes. So I cannot ..."

"Oh, that's all right. My treat."

"He will be waiting outside Woolworth shop. We must not be too close."

She lifted the bag. This time, Billy insisted on taking it off her and threw it over his shoulder. But Sofia grabbed it back forcefully.

"No! No!"

She moved forwards 10 metres and then motioned for him to follow. She headed towards the upended jaw of the whale that overlooks the town. She half-turned and asked what it was. Billy told her about the whaling industry in Victorian times.

"I am glad they stop! It is not good."

Keeping a dozen steps between them, they descended into the spectacular deep-cut valley of the Khyber Pass. From here, it was a stone's throw to the slipway that led down to the beach. The tide was on its way out and the dog skidded on the concrete brushed with sand. Sofia turned sharp left and led them under the dark, overhanging cliffs. She stopped, scanned around and then beckoned them to come closer.

"No one see us here. I rush, so I can spend more time." She took a deep, long breath and looked out to sea. "I wish I was at home."

Billy said the first thing that came into his head. "How come you speak such good English?"

"Oh, my father make us go to extra lessons. He like the English very much."

"What does he do?"

"He is ... I do not know how you say ... with land?"

"A farmer?"

"Yes. Farmer. Big farm, mountains like this."

She pointed at the cliff. Billy couldn't believe his luck. She was a country girl.

"But then, our land is not good ... they came ..."

"They?"

She clammed up and bit her lip.

"I tell you another time. It is too nice now. Too nice to tell you bad stories of Albania."

They strolled along, sometimes throwing a stick for the dog or lingering to look at a starfish. She was sixteen, born in the same year as him, and she liked everything to do with nature. They were so alike, apart from the fact she was a Cancer and had never heard of rugby. Folk dance was her one real passion. That's why she had been so drawn to the monument that day.

All too soon, they arrived where the long plate-glass window of the Pavilion overlooked the beach. Billy called the dog and put her on the lead, but there was no time for coffee. Sofia was becoming uneasy again.

"Billy, I must go. But I must see you again. Tomorrow."

"Yes ... that would be great ... er ..."

"Yes, I have to see you. Same place?"

"Same place!"

"Please promise to be here."

"I promise, course I do."

"Please, there is something ..."

To his amazement, she turned, moved square in front of him and kissed him hard on the cheek.

"You are my only friend in England."

She knelt on the sand to give Twiggy a final hug then sped off towards the steps that were gouged into the steep grassy slope. Billy was in shock. In all his sixteen years, no one had shown him so much affection. I have to see you! he thought. Not want to, or would like to see you ... have to!

He walked back along the beach, king of all he surveyed. It was a good week now, not a boring one. Terry Thwaites was an OK bloke, not just a past-it musician who was full of himself. It was great that Mother was home from France again, great she had met him. Morris dancing was a fine way to spend a holiday. He would ring Nan later and actually believe what he was telling her.

Love changes the world. At the ice-cream stall, Billy bought a 99 and gave Twiggy the Flake. He strode off in the direction of the caravan whistling *Richmond Hill*. He liked it now.

Wednesday morning began very much as the day before. They were both exactly on time. She smiled faintly and set off down the steps ahead of them. As soon as they reached the beach, Twiggy was let go. She chased gulls along the surf line, trying to pilfer their scraps of food.

They ambled along like any other young couple, although the slender, high-cheekboned girl might have been a supermodel and he a plumber's mate. She sketched in bits of her life as they walked.

The folk festival was very like the one she and Maria performed at every year at Peshkopia. They really had won prizes.

"You must be very good."

"I do not think so. It is, what you say? Fashion now in my country. Since independence, everyone play old music, everyone sing old songs."

Billy described his moment of glory on the rugby field when he, a prop not a pansy fly-half, drop-kicked a goal to win a schools trophy. She tried to look impressed. It was idyllic: the sun, the sparkling sea, the children playing ... then her mood changed.

"Billy, I want tell you about my friend. Uncle Luan does not let me see her or call her."

"Your friend? Maria? Weird, isn't it? When you think that's why you came here ..." She stopped and took a torn-off corner of paper from the side panel of her purse. "I think this is address ..."

"What?"

"Where she live. Last week, I hear him shouting at someone on phone. He leave door open and I see him. It is locked most always. I can only ring Papa when he is standing by me. I am sure he said 'Maria', I am sure he was talking to her. He say her father owe him money. Then he shout at her to give Mehmet something ... he is so angry, I have never seen Uncle Luan so angry. Then he is writing and break pencil. He put phone down and slam door. I hide in bathroom, so he not see me. And for first time, he forget to lock door ... I go in and do this."

She demonstrated the old trick of rubbing a pencil over an indentation to get an image. Sure enough, an address showed up like a brass rubbing. An address in Middlesbrough.

"I did not know how to find number. I look in directory. But I was frightened he come back soon. Then I find it ... 1471, and I ring, but it said the caller did not give number. I only have this." She was close to tears. "But I know it was my friend. He said Maria! He said Maria give Mehmet something!"

"But why don't you just ask him? Why don't you just say I need to talk to her."

"Ha! I ask many time, but he say she busy."

"Then I think it's time you told the police."

"Polici? He say it will be bad for her and bad for me. He say there is a problem with papers and we just have to be patient until they are through or I am in big trouble. And if I am sent home, what will happen to Maria Pladici? She will be alone and I will let down Papa. We have no money and there is agreement, things we must do. Then Luan say everything is fine. But he keep me like this, he keep passport. And if he go out on business Mehmet come and sit by the door. He is very strange ... so I am always watched. I can do nothing ... nothing ..."

"Then I'll tell the police for you."

"No. Please listen what I say! He will know. Billy, you are my friend now ... will you do something for me?"

"Yes, of course."

"I see map in library. Middlesbrough very near. There is many bus every day. You will go to this place? Find out if she is there? Tell her I want to see her. Sofia want to see her!"

Billy thought for a moment, trying to understand what was going on.

"Well ... I can try."

"Tell her I am here in England now and what is happening. How Luan keep me and not let me ring Papa. She will know what to do. She will come for me."

She was on the point of breaking down again. Billy looked around nervously.

"OK. I'll go and see what I can find out. Middlesbrough, you say?"

"Yes. Tomorrow we meet at station. I will show you where it is. We can make arrangements. Next day you go find her. Please help me, Billy."

A north-east chill blew off the sea, the first reminder that summer really was coming to an end. Sofia drew her blouson collar up around her neck and they walked along the beach in silence, until they reached the steps.

"Tomorrow, Billy ... eleven. Please promise you will be there. By station." She took hold of both of his hands and looked him in the eye. "Promise!"

"I'll be there."

She gave his hands a final lingering squeeze, looked up at the cliff and then turned and ran away, her shoulder bag jumping up and down on her back.

"Twiggy! Here girl!"

The dog was all but forgotten. She was crunching up the remains of an ice cream cone, when she heard a distant whistle echoing off the cliffs. She sensed something was amiss. As she came to Billy's side, he was staring out to sea.

"Don't even know where it is. And what will I do with you for a whole day?"

They took the well-trodden route back to the caravan.

Once back, Billy settled Twiggy down with a biscuit, a sure sign he was going straight out. He took the half-chewed map of Whitby from the TV unit where Nan had left it. The library was more than handy, just opposite the station.

Half an hour later, he was pushing through the swing barrier to the enquiry desk. He could hardly believe his eyes – the assistant was none other than the dowdy lady from his morris team. She looked at him disdainfully. She had not forgotten the lazy-limbed youth, who had ruined the performance in front of her assembled friends. He blushed the most volcanic, most unstoppable blush ever. Then he garbled his enquiry in such a way as to confirm her opinion of him. Nevertheless, she directed him with the cold efficiency of a dyed in the wool librarian.

He soon found a Cadogan Guide to England under 'Travel'. It was the very same edition Nan had borrowed before they came away. Nan liked to know exactly what she was letting herself in for. He sat down at an ink-tattooed desk as far away from the counter as possible and thumbed to the index clumsily. Middlesbrough was allocated but half a page. It said: the only reason to go into the city is the transporter bridge ...

Just my luck! Billy thought. The day trip to hell ...

Despite his embarrassment, he darted back and forth to the desk several times. He found a town centre map in the local information section and managed, after three attempts, to get a reasonable photocopy of it. He chased up every snippet of information about Middlesbrough that he could, until a sepia photograph of the said famous bridge somehow jogged his memory. Wasn't he supposed to be meeting Mother outside the Sutcliffe shop at one thirty? Wasn't it today they were going to see Terry's new venture, the shanty boat? He'd been so taken over by other matters; Mother had taken a back seat. He thudded the tome on Middlesbrough Bridge Builders shut, raced to the counter and slammed it on the desk. The librarian gurned in disgust.

She caressed the book and then carried it sedately back to the local history shelf like it was the Crown Jewels.

Billy was already five minutes late, though he knew it probably wouldn't matter.

It didn't. Mother turned up ten minutes after him.

"Where's Terry?"

"He's already there, love. I had to go to the chemist for some paracetamol."

They scurried along over the bridge into Church Street and then on to Tate Hill. Mother disappeared down a narrow alleyway. At the very end, she knocked on the door of a toytown cottage with glass floats in nets hanging outside. It belonged to Ted Morris and it backed directly onto the beach.

"Come through, Corinne. It's you, is it … Billy Elliot?"

The joke had worn thin by now.

Ted led them down a narrow corridor into the kitchen. The back door was open; the smell of ozone was overpowering.

"There he is. Blackbeard and his new flag ship."

They could see Terry wobbling about in a clapped-out four-seater dinghy. You couldn't swing a ship's cat in it, never mind seat a crew of shanty singers. His straggly beard and bushy hair wafted in the breeze, while his enormous hanging beer belly swung from side to side. Mother and Billy scrambled down a collapsed sea wall onto the sand.

"Welcome aboard, landlubbers. Ha-har!"

He spoke in mock pirate. Some local anglers, descendants of generations of whalers no doubt, watched from a wharf nearby. They shook their heads and smirked. Billy was embarrassed, but Terry carried on imposing his sense of humour on the seafaring world.

"And you be officially press-ganged now, my lad!"

Mother laughed uproariously.

"Do you do art at school?"

"No."

"Tech drawing?"

"No."

"Great. You're ideal for this job then!"

Heidi Smart had made a stencil for Terry to paint onto the bows. He was too ham-fisted to do the work himself, so he wanted Billy to do it –

he was attempting to be inclusive. Billy realised that and so felt obliged. He got as far as 'S-C-R-A', when Mother decided to take over. He was painfully slow. It was his chance to excuse himself. He had to attend to Twiggy. He had nothing in for tea. No he didn't want to go to Terry's for a barbie in the yard. He clambered up onto the old jetty and just managed to get away before Terry broke into Haul away, heave away! We're bound for South Australia!

7

Albania to Albion

One thing was certain – there were always Zanders in the valley. No one could say when they first came. In the graveyard, Zander headstones were grander, more numerous than any other familys. They survived the Ottomans, corrupt kings, blood feuds, Serbian overlords, world wars ... They had managed to keep themselves and half the village fed. Their farm was always the best run. They bred the finest horses to plough the hard, stony land. Zanders were, by tradition, Bektashi, religious people – wise and God-fearing. They dealt fairly with one and all. They had been aldermen, mayors, pillars of the community. They were the essence of Albania. Each new Zander inherited his land, his faith and his history, secure in the knowledge that land, faith and history would carry on as ever. As the past, so the future. Mere governments would never change that.

Not long before the Second World War, King Zog cosied up to Mussolini, the man who rebuilt Rome. 'Il Duce' became his wise benefactor. He offered friendship in a friendless world, then advice, then material aid. He was so generous – he adorned modest little Albanian towns with fine buildings. But, in the fine tradition of Roman Emperors, the fine buildings turned out to be Trojan Horses; an effective means with which to take over the whole country. No one noticed, until the guest became the landlord. Zog escaped by the skin of his teeth, helped by British intelligence; a certain Ian Fleming (who never wrote a James Bond thriller as far-fetched as this).

In 1940, Stefan Zander joined the resistance – such as it was. Many had become collaborators; there was more in it for them. He blew up bridges, threw grenades into brothels, made ravines impassable and streets hostile. And when the Germans came to shore things up, while others cried 'Welcome', he warmed their backsides with mines. He sought out the British SOE agents dropped by moonlight to incite rebellion. He sheltered them, fed them, tended them when they were injured. He held the Kanan dear – the ancient code of hospitality by which a man is judged. Where matters of honour are concerned, Albanians are the most generous people on earth. They are the best of friends, the worst of enemies.

The British agents seemed to be like them: brave, honourable; they might have been Bektashi in their own country. He trusted their word. He trusted Mr Churchill. The exiled king would be restored, peace and democracy installed.

So Stefan's cell fought recklessly, impossibly hard. When it was all over, the victory parade done, the rose petals brushed off their shoulders, they gathered in the village square … and were shot. They were the wrong kind of resistance; royalists, not communists. Stefan was lucky – he was lambing that day. Work always came first.

Albania was delivered up like a reluctant bride to a wicked baron. A wicked Russian baron called Stalin. The 'Land of the Eagle' became 'The People's Republic of Albania'. From that day, Stefan's tale could not be told outside his own four walls.

Zog never returned. He wiled away his days in the London Ritz, having emptied the state coffers before he went. As Stefan said, "When the eagle flew, he took the nest-egg with him!"

So he went back to his farming, ploughing the rough slopes, scything the meagre hay. He found himself a wife, a distant cousin who could be trusted, and settled down like generations of Albanians before him, saying nothing, simply waiting for this latest political fad, Communism, to end. And so it did. But before it did, it managed to do what nothing else had. It took their faith, their history and their way of life and mangled them into an unrecognisable heap. Why? Because in 1946, one particularly ambitious and wily official. Enver Hoxha, made himself Prime Minister. Soon after, he declared Albania to be an atheist state. No more Gods. Even Russia did not go that far. What are Christianity and Islam? Opiates. And those self-important Bektashis? Charlatans … they contribute nothing to the people. What is this so-called 'history'? A catalogue of corrupt kings and capitalist exploitation. The slate must be wiped clean. The day the communists took over was the day Albania's history began.

Soon after, thirteen smiling commissars came to Stefan's farm with measuring tapes and clipboards. It turned out to be his Doomsday. The land was to be 'requisitioned' for the state. The valley was the ideal site for a steelworks. A 'five-year plan' was set in motion. Stefan Zander's best land was taken. He was allowed to keep a few scrubby acres above the farm, where the mountain goats clung to the cliffs, but what would be left for Gjergi, his newborn son? Every time he stepped out of the door he saw giant diggers eating his inheritance away. They had a keen sense of humour, those thirteen smiling commissars.

After a few months, he could no longer bear to look. He could no longer stand the smoke, the slag heaps, the encroaching shadows, the screeching bogies pulling coal and ore. It was a gaping vision of hell.

Then, all in a day, the Russians went. Word was out in the village: Stalin has died. What does this mean? Was there a glimmer of hope? For a few fleeting hours, while the old men played dominoes and sipped their Turkish coffee, perhaps there was. But Hoxha the wise, Hoxha the all-seeing, deemed that Stalin had not been Stalinist enough. He invited the Chinese to replace him. In much the same way Zog embraced Mussolini, Hoxha embraced Mao Zedong. It was the embrace of the dragon.

Soon, a delegation of blue-boiler-suited, little-red-book-waving officials were coming up the hill. Stefan gave them tea and they relieved him of the last of the high meadows. It was the final straw.

"Does this Mao Zedong really need a dozen Albanian goats?" he asked.

He was too old to be afraid of consequences. It seemed they did, as long as they were communist goats.

Stefan retreated to the kitchen, sat on the pile of pine logs by the brazier, took out his yellowing Bektashi manuscripts and prepared for the next life.

Sometimes, his wife got him to do a household repair or to cut herbs from the kitchen garden, but he worked like a zombie. He had lost the heart for it.

"Let them have it, let it rot. God will punish."

She never came to terms with the land grabs, the plans, the betrayals, the forced labours. She cursed and complained every day. He grew old quickly and passed away bowing to the fate God had given.

Poor little Gjergi was left with a barren fraction of the ancestral land. It couldn't feed a dog, let alone him and a sick mother. For the next eight years, they barely survived. As soon as he was old enough, he took government work far away in Tropoja, shovelling concrete into a bunker; countless were built to warn off 'enemies of the state'. He caught the eye of a beautiful young peasant girl. She was wearing the traditional garb – the embroidered tunic with tassels, the Turkish shoes, the draped headdress. She was unusually fair-skinned, almost albino.

"Want to buy a nice new bunker?" he joked.

"We have enough of our own," she replied.

"We keep shit in them."

They married before they really knew each other. They had to.

Village folk were suspicious when he brought Anna home, the odd-looking girl from the north. 'White witch', they called her. His mother set her to work, testing her out with the hardest, dirtiest jobs. But she was honest, settled quickly and within five years she bore Gjergi three sons: Kristo, Luan and Mihal. The oldest and the youngest were much alike, as is often the case. They grew into stout, uncomplicated boys, with a natural nobility of bearing like Grandfather Stefan. They got on well at school; accepted their fate. In fact, they were so well regarded they became leaders in the local Communist Youth.

After 1,000 years, the Bektashi strand was broken.

The middle brother Luan was another matter. He inherited all of the bitterness and none of the wisdom. His grandmother doted on him and she called him 'wolf cub'. He was impatient with history; injustice stung him every day. He couldn't walk up the winding road to the farm without spitting on the monument by the Bluewater Spring. A couple of communist 'heroes' had been shot there, but there was no mention of the six royalists, who had fallen in the same action. He mocked his father for accepting his lot. He scoffed at his past as a 'government slave'.

"Father, how is it you spend your time whittling pegs, while all around us the government steals?"

He had fire in his belly. The fact grandfather was a resistance hero meant nothing; they had won the war and lost the peace. What use was that? Here he was, 15 years old, a Zander in his own land, trudging up to the site office to beg for a job in the very rolling mill that had dispossessed him. He resented every shovelful of coke.

It fell on Kristo, being the eldest, to tend to the 'farm'. Well, three fields and a chicken run. Young Mihal was soon forced into the steel mill, too, to the very same section as his brother. No one picked on the shy boy while Luan Zander was around. He was a foot taller than the average Albanian, with dark, brooding eyes.

On the weekends, Luan didn't attend the rallies. He turned his mind to other things. He found ways to make an extra lek or two. Albania happens to be a very small country, all coastline and boundaries. Much of it is rugged, inhospitable, too wild to police, even for the most dedicated communist. In some places, you're more likely to see a bear than a person. He began to take a peculiar interest in fishing, in hunting, in those very country pursuits he had despised in his father. He went to stay in Tropoja with his mother's relatives, but it was not fish or fur that they were bringing in. Jeans, drink, razors, soap, records and scent filled the boot of his cousin's rickety saloon. And the family, though aware of this, said nothing. Many sons did exactly the same. It made life bearable. You see, the communist system, for all its ideology, all its control of resources, all its planning down to the last rivet, could not make a decent pair of jeans. Denim brought it down, not tanks. And Luan, despite his lack of years and schooling, saw this was the case. While others despaired, cowered under the overbearing, soulless might of 'the system', he knew the truth; it was as rotten as a lice-infested old shed. And he was right. After Mao died in 1976, the Chinese knot was loosened and the system began to crumble and lean. Strange how the removal of one small, fat man can change the fate of a nation. Young Luan was tailor-made for what was to follow. He had all the makings of a self-made man.

Ancient property deeds were salvaged from tin boxes hidden in outhouses and eventually, after four decades, the Zanders got their land back. But this was of no use to Luan, for Kristo stood to inherit the farm. Anyway, much of it was so poisoned it would never produce in his lifetime.

But then fate stepped in to twist the knife. Gjergi was faced with a mountain of work overnight. And work he did ... to a standstill. In all hours, in all weathers, he strove to restore the land and put things right. He died of pneumonia a year and a day after the freedom celebrations. Soon after, his embittered wife was found in the Bluewater stream. Some say it was suicide.

A family meeting was called; not that there was much to discuss. Kristo would carry on with the farm. Mihal would help – he was willing and liked to build. They would stay put and make a go of things. Luan would be given what small amount of money they had saved and would take himself off to Tirana. He had friends there in business. He would apprentice himself to a clothing firm. He was happy enough. He was not destined to be a peasant farmer.

Life went on with back-breaking work and a half-empty table. Mihal grew strong on it. But, unexpectedly, Mihal, who could wrestle a bear, Mihal, who had taken a particular delight in demolishing the steelwork sheds that had blighted their land, contracted cancer. Asbestosis, they said. The communist curse lived on. A lion of a man was laid low by dust. There was no question of compensation. Kristo grieved for a day, then carried on …

"Cows have to be milked …"

Despite man's abuses, nature clawed its way back. Kristo marvelled as the land self-healed and centimetre by square centimetre it became productive again. Even the pelicans came home to nest amongst the rotting pylons. Wild flowers, not seen since the steel mill, sprang up along the lanes. Old women picked the *lule basani* and *kulumbria* and made their potions. Green is the colour of hope.

Kristo worked on with little time for leisure. He was well past thirty before he married and that only came about through friends in the village. They set him up with a raggedy girl from a farm in the high mountains. She would have married anyone with a roof and a tap. He looked much older than his bride and people thought he was her father. But they got on well, she made few demands on him and she was as strong and as willing as he could wish for.

By the time Luan came home after years of little news, they had a daughter, Sofia.

"You are an uncle, Luan! The Zanders live on!"

She was born with snow-white hair and deep azure eyes. Just like Grandma Anna. They doted on her. Luan had changed. He looked foreign. He sported an Armani suit, smelled of expensive Italian aftershave and drove a brand new BMW, which he'd got from Germany. He was an exporter and spent much of his time in Belgium and England. He took a shine to his new niece, plied her with presents, dolls from America, her first 'make-up kit', top-brand trainers. The better business was, the better the presents.

"And what is it you export, Luan?" Kristo asked.

"Anything they want!" Luan replied, laughing. "The world is an oyster, they say, brother, and I am a pearl diver!"

From then on, he came several times a year, until Sofia was in her teens. They could hardly wait for his visits. When he arrived, they ran down the path to meet him. Meanwhile, Kristo struggled to make the farm pay. He missed Mihal desperately, but could not afford an extra pair of hands. Albanian produce could not compete with the mountains that Euroland piled high and left to rot. Freedom brought a subsistence life, no more.

He did ensure one thing: Sofia, precious Sofia, had the very best education. And he made sure she learned English, not Italian; much more the done thing. Not just because it would open the doors to the world, but because he remembered grandfather's tales of the English gentlemen, who had come in the war and laid their lives down. Albanians have long memories. Every year on Independence Day, November the twenty-eighth, they took the girl to the British cemetery at Tirana. A particular friend of Grandfather Stefan was buried there.

"He was shot in the back," Kristo always said after the wreath was laid. "... by the communists."

Mama made Sofia learn the traditional music as she had done. It was an extra string to the bow.

"People always want music," she reasoned. "No matter how bad things are."

Sofia joined a local village troupe. She made many friends. Her best friend was Maria Pladici. They were so good, they formed a duet and played at weddings, parties, birthdays ... They won prizes every year at Oda Dibrana. One year, Luan came all the way from Bruges to see them perform. He was so impressed, he took them to his flat in Tirana to show them off to his business friends. Everywhere they went they were fêted.

"Ah, Maria Pladici can sing, but the Zander girl ... you can see the Bektashi in her. That certain look in the eye."

Indeed, she was famous for those piercing blue eyes and albino looks ... and for the traditional costumes her mother painstakingly sewed. With every delicate stitch of shining red and black silk, the story of Albania was passed on, cocking a snook at systems, whatever they were. With every note of music, the old ways were celebrated. In Albania, they don't take their culture for granted. In Albania, they dance their morris with pride.

Life might be hard, but Kristo was thankful. He had not suffered like Stefan, or Gjergi. Who would have believed he would vote for his own government one day? And the land, the precious earth, however polluted, however darkened by the pall of history, was his again.

And things were going to get much better. Luan brought Sofia a present for her sixteenth birthday – a pink pull-along trunk full of fashionable clothes from London! How they stood round picking them up, trying them on. How could she ever wear fake labels again? She would pile them up in the yard and burn them!

"This is the most wonderful day of my life! Real Nike, Papa!"

After several bottles of wine, the best Shesi e Zi they had tasted for years, Luan stood up, tapped the side of his glass and announced that he now owned his very own business in England.

"You know the old saying? Never work on someone else's farm! I have a proposition!"

Many Albanians already worked for him, but he really needed someone who could speak good English, a translator who was reliable and who could represent the firm. Who better than someone from his own family? Who better than Sofia? Oh, and had they heard? Maria Pladici had left her job as a secretary in the hospital in Shkodra and was going to work for him in England. Ah, Maria ... Sofia wondered why she hadn't been in touch.

"Why waste your talent, niece?" asked Luan, with an appealing spread of his arms. "There is no work in Albania. And remember the pyramid schemes? Is that our idea of good investment? No, Sofia! Do what everyone else is doing. Go abroad for a time and make your fortune there. Then come back and Papa can have the new cow shed, clear the scrub and weeds, buy more sheep, buy more land ... buy the mountains!"

As the night wore on, Luan convinced Kristo that his daughter was destined for greater things. She could make barrow loads of money and send it home. Everyone was doing it. There was no need to worry about documents. No need to worry about fares. The business would attend to everything. All she had to do was to pack up her posh new suitcase and go. Of course, there was no pressure. He would give her, say, two weeks to make her mind up, before he advertised the post in the *Tirana Free Press*.

"See sense, brother. She'll bring good fortune to you."

They laughed and hugged, and then Luan got into his swish car and drove off down the mountainside, peeping his horn as he went. What a man! What a kind, brilliant man!

Sofia took to her next English lessons with a new relish. She read everything she could about England. England, where Jane Austen characters lived prosperous lives in pastoral bliss. Her mind was quickly made up.

8

Bus Rides and Blue Tape

As Sofia approached the station, she saw Billy looking at the timetable on the wall. She had told Luan she was going to the Ladies in the concourse, though he was suspicious. These days, he would not let her out of his sight for more than a few minutes. He'd even confiscated her suitcase the evening before and handed out clothes that morning like dispensing charity.

She coughed loudly to attract Billy's attention then, with a slight pushing motion of her hand, she warned him to keep his distance. He got the message and stood where he was. She pretended to be checking the timetable farther down, but edged gradually towards him. When they were side by side, she pressed a screwed up note into his hand. She turned quickly round. Luan was gesticulating from across the road. She dropped a small, lavender envelope and edged away again. Billy slid his foot over it then pretended to drop his wallet, so he could pick the two things up at once. 'Maria Pladici' was scrawled across one side, with something in Albanian on the other. By now, Sofia was standing some way off and was watching from the corner of her eye. She nodded twice and then dodged between the queues of cars to join Luan. They ran off down Windsor Road like the devil was chasing them.

Billy waited until they had disappeared into the crowds then went to an old-fashioned telephone booth in the station, where he phoned Mother's mobile.

"Mother … I'm nearby … just to let you know I'm on my way to see you … about half an hour … no, just being social … but I'm on the way now …"

Before Mother had the chance to refuse, he hooked up the phone. He stood thinking for a moment. If he could be bothered to pick up the dog, it would be worth it; the two of them wouldn't be made welcome for long. He opened out the note – it was the address in

Middlesbrough, written in bold capitals. He slid it into the deepest side pocket of his body warmer, the security one that zipped up. He had a last look at the envelope and put that in an inside pocket. He took a few minutes to mooch round the station and bus depot, so he would know exactly where the bus went from, then set off for the caravan. He'd worked out a new short cut from the town centre to the campsite. It passed right by Terry's cottage.

But to save precious time, he risked going that way. He crouched like a hunchback as he passed under the window. Terry's favourite Watersons' album was blaring out at full blast.

By the time he was racing back down the hill, a thick sea mist had descended and the harbour was barely visible. Terry opened the door in garish tartan shorts and his 'Real Ale/Real Man' T-shirt.

"See you've brought your own dog of the scrawny variety, wor Billy!"

Billy squeezed past him into the living room. Twiggy stopped to sniff Terry's feet obsessively. Mother was laid out on the well-worn Chesterfield sofa, wrapped in an outsize man's dressing gown.

"William, love! Keep control of the dog in here, will you?"

Billy reeled her in and perched on the end of the arm.

"I've just come to let you know we're walking the Cleveland Way tomorrow. So I probably won't see you. Maybe going the whole way to Robin Hood's Bay."

"The whole way? It's longer than you think, hinny!" Terry said.

"We can get the bus back."

"You wish. It's a longer and harder walk than it looks on the map. They've found skeletons along that path! Robin Hood's Bay. I used to run the folk club there for years. Yeah, that was where we did the first gig with Drunk Willy –"

Billy jumped in before Terry could start the Drunk Willy chapter of his life.

"Well, perhaps we'll only go so far then."

"Just be sensible. Get the forecast first and ring us later on to let us know you're all right."

"Will do, Mother. I'll be off, then!"

"Off? You came all this way just to tell us that? You could have said that on the phone, William. Anyway, you may as well stay for some lunch."

"Er ... no ... I've got some tokens for a McDonald's. May as well use them."

Bus Rides and Blue Tape

"But you've only been here five minutes."
"Sorry. I've got a few things to do."
"Well, do as you please."

Billy took a long, long detour to the other side of town, to the area where Sofia lived. He felt safe in the sea fog that seemed to be getting worse by the hour. When he passed by the end of her terrace, he turned his collar up like a spy. Twiggy whimpered as if she recognised the place or remembered the scent. She was in such a panic that morning, Billy thought, perhaps I ought to just knock on the door.

He lingered near the launderette for a few seconds. Then it came back to him what she had said and how he had promised to do only what she wanted. He shook his head and walked on.

"I must be mad! Going to a place I don't know, trying to find a person I don't know, for some reason I don't know, because someone I don't know asked me to."

At least Mother had left him to his own devices. She was now living in a time warp with self-proclaimed folk legend Terry Thwaites, formerly of Scrawny Dog, Drunk Willy and any number of stupidly named bands. So he was justified in doing exactly what he wanted.

"I'll just treat it as a day out, that's all," he said out loud to himself. "Just a day out and no one will ever know a thing about it."

The next morning, Billy woke early. He was washed, dressed and breakfasted by six. He shut the dog in his room so he could arrange things without hindrance. First, he placed several saucers of water around the kitchenette. Feeding was going to be the real problem. Twiggy would wolf down seven meals in one sitting given the chance. She had no concept of breakfast, lunch, evening meal, supper. He had an idea. If he hid half a dozen chew sticks around the caravan, that would provide her with a challenge. If one took, say, half an hour to finish, six would keep her occupied for the best part of the morning. She normally slept through afternoons anyway so, if the buses ran true, he would be back just in time to ring Nan at five or for any teatime visits from Mother.

"Huh! If she bothers ..."

He made sure every door that could be shut was shut and every chewable object was put out of reach. He split the *Daily Express* Nan had left and spread it over the kitchen floor. Then, to burn up at least some of her excessive energy, he took Twiggy round three circuits of the site. When they got back, he tied her to a standpipe outside, while he made a final check round.

Everything that could be done was done. It was eight and time to go. He tugged her inside and let her off the lead. He ordered her to sit, wait, beg and then handed her a ghoulish dried pig's ear. She took it to her basket, lodged it between her paws and began to gnaw contentedly.

"Good girl, good girl," he repeated and edged out of the door.

He turned the lock gently, took a last look through the lounge window and set off down the track.

The last bank holiday of the year was over. It was September the second, only seven days before the new term, and streams of people were plodding into town, like hunched figures in a Lowry painting.

By the time Billy got to the bus station it was heaving. Fathers struggled with luggage, mothers dragged screaming toddlers behind them and old folks peered at the timetables at point-blank range. There was that distinct feeling of 'summer over, back to drudgery' in the air.

Billy took his place in the queue for the 93 bus to Middlesbrough. He was getting the eight forty-five to give himself as much leeway as possible. He was travelling light, relying on his body warmer to carry everything he needed. He had borrowed a plastic pouch from his RSPB pack to keep the scrawled address in, even though he had committed it to memory. He had a photocopied map of Middlesbrough rolled up in an inside pocket and the letter Sofia gave him was slotted into the back section of his wallet. That was lodged tight in the zip-up pocket.

People started getting on the bus and the queue shuffled forwards. As he stepped onto the platform, the point of no return, Billy felt a sudden urge to back out. He steeled himself, paid the driver for a day return and took a place directly behind the special seats for the elderly.

As the bus drew laboriously out of town, Billy looked back. Whitby was again completely shrouded in sea mist, with the odd gable end, gazebo or Victorian chimney jutting through. It looked even more like the set of a horror film.

Soon, they were driving over the purple, late summer heather of the moors. The mist gave way to a brilliant blue sky, not a cloud or vapour trail to sully it. Sometimes, ranks of Forestry Commission trees marched over the horizon. It was a broad-brush landscape on a canvas with no edge. The land tilted towards the sea as if trying to topple them in, but soon the sea was out of sight altogether. The scenery was beautifully bleak, as empty as anywhere in England. Occasional hints of past endeavour showed up: a milestone, a fallen wall, a grassy track.

There were very few stops among the broad, mottled slopes. After three-quarters of an hour, they were coming sharply down off the Cleveland Hills, looking into the Tees Valley. There was a mist there, too, but this hung as a yellow pall. What did that old book in the library say? '... once the most beautiful estuary in England. It teemed with salmon and trout that spawned in the pure waters of the Pennines ...'

Salmon teemed no longer. There were no meadows full of cowslip and gentian now. Nature was suffocated under a mishmash of Victorian back-to-backs, decaying factories and sixties estates, all trussed round by pylons and pipeline. Billy sighed. If nothing else, he had learned some geography. Middlesbrough, it seems, like Crewe or Swindon, had come into being for one particular reason – trains; in this case the Stockton and Darlington Railway Company. It was the port at the end of the line. A place to take the coal from. Ironstone was discovered in the nearby hills, so blast furnaces followed, then steel, chemicals, engineering – all in the wake of the railway. The Tees was ingeniously bridged and to cut a long story short, the Teesside engineers went on to bridge the rivers of the world: the Sydney Harbour, the Menai Strait, the Nile, the Limpopo, the Severn, the Zambezi – all spanned by Middlesbrough graft.

He knew what to expect, but after the glinting sea, the mist, and the moors, it still came as a shock. Within an hour and a half, Billy had gone from a quaint seaside resort to an urban free-for-all. The Cleveland Hills looked like a distant Shangri-La.

The 93 bus was sucked into the rush-hour traffic; the natural sounds of this habitat were screeching brakes and cursing drivers. Billy got out of his seat well before the bus came to a halt and swayed to the front like a sailor on a rough sea. The automatic door rattled open and he jumped out. He had the now very crinkled photocopied map ready in his hand. He kept checking it as he dodged behind the queues and out of the station.

He realised he was in a square named after Captain Cook. It seemed he was everywhere. On another day, it might have been a reassuring presence. He sat down on a concrete seat stuccoed by pigeon droppings and took out his pocket diary. He cross-referenced the route he'd listed with the map then sighted the landmarks immediately around him. He wanted to avoid wasting time or bothering people, to find his way in and out as quickly as he could. After two minutes he'd got his bearings exactly – the Captain would have been proud.

He quickly gathered his things up and set off again, this time with a confident step. He was at the shopping centre within seconds and Linthorpe Road within minutes. From here, it looked only a short stretch from Southfield to the university district, where he'd circled one particular side street in red biro.

His pace was modest, yet he was sweating rivulets. His rugby shirt stuck to his back like he was in a tough match, but he pressed on, ignoring the discomfort. Within half an hour he was at the end of the very street he wanted. It seemed all too easy.

It was a Victorian terrace of grand houses, no doubt built for those entrepreneurs and pioneers who invented a city from nothing. Some in the row were obvious student flats – Billy could tell by the bin bags full of wine bottles, the unkempt front gardens, the blu-tacked posters on unwashed windows. For all that, the houses had a friendly aura. Others in the row showed a more unwelcome face to the world. Their decadence was of a sinister nature: number forty-one had no roof, number forty-nine had no windows, fifty-nine was burnt out, and sixty-three was derelict. Billy walked along warily, checking each door as he went by ... sixty-seven, sixty-nine, seventy-one, seventy-three ... almost there ... But as he approached seventy-five, he noticed blue-and-white tape stretched across the front gate. It was fluttering in the breeze.

'Police. Do not cross' was written at intervals.

A policeman was standing in the porch entrance. His hands were clasped behind his back and he was as still as a statue. Billy checked the piece of paper Sofia had given him – seventy-five ... this was definitely it ...

By now, the policeman had noticed him. Mona Lisa eyes were following him as he went so Billy crossed to the other side of the street. The tape was stretched from the racing green gatepost to a laburnum stump in the corner of the garden, then along a crumbling boundary wall to the edge of the window. There, it was weighed down carelessly by a brick on the sill. Another length was stretched across a side entry under an arch. The front door was open. Billy slowed almost to a standstill. He could just make out the profile of another policeman at the end of a long corridor. He was placing clothing into a plastic bag, while talking to someone in matter-of-fact tones. Billy carried on to the end of the street, which fizzled out into abandoned allotments. He turned, somewhat embarrassed, and made his way back, determined to get a closer look. As he drew near a second time, he shouted across to the policeman.

"Excuse me, is that where Mr Threadgold lives?"

"Threadgold? You've got the wrong address, my lad."

"I'm sure it's his address ... it is seventy-five, isn't it?" Billy asked as he crossed the road.

"Yes. Er ... don't come near the tape, lad, you might contaminate the evidence."

"Evidence?"

"Please move on, you've got the wrong address."

Billy was at a loss. Perhaps it was the right time to declare his hand, tell the policeman he was looking for someone. He slowed almost to a stop, as if the burden of deciding what to do was too much to bear.

A student happened to be watching from number thirty-eight across the road. In fact, she'd been watching number seventy-five for quite some time. She forced open a heavy sash window – it screeched and rattled. Billy looked up. A distinctly punkish girl shouted down to him.

"Are the police still there?"

"Yes."

"I saw you hanging around. I wouldn't go anywhere near that place if I were you."

"Er ... I was visiting someone."

"Visiting someone at seventy-five? Are you kidding? Hang on a sec."

Her face disappeared. Billy wished he had kept his mouth shut. She clattered downstairs and swung the door open.

"Are you from the student mag?"

"No." He was flattered to be asked. He was big for his age, but not the least bit studenty. "I was checking something out for a friend."

"Oh God! You're not one of those are you?"

A look of utter disgust crumpled her face.

"What do you mean?"

"One of those mindless sexist pigs exploiting those poor girls."

"Pardon?"

"OK, I must warn you – it's us who got it sorted out. The Union. We oppose people trafficking in all its forms. Especially under-aged girls.

We're sick of what's been happening round here. Some of them were only fourteen, those bah-stards."

Billy had just met his first student union rep, Kate Henderson-Pullar. She was the Women's Officer. Where there were 'issues', there was HP.

"I'm not sure what you mean, but I only came to find someone …"

She was fiendishly intelligent. She'd been on University Challenge before she was thrown out of her first college. She quickly assessed that Billy was too young and too fresh-faced to be a customer.

"Honestly, I was looking for someone … Maria Pladici … my friend in Whitby asked me to find out what was going on."

"Your friend? You mean you actually know someone who was in there?"

"Well, not me. My friend does. They came from Albania for a job."

"A job! That's rich."

"A translator."

"Ha! Translator!"

"Yes. I said I would come to see what was going on, that's all. She was concerned."

"You're a day too late. When the police raid eventually happened, like months after we first warned them, the main culprits had gone. Someone seems to have tipped them off. There were five girls … I mean girls … they took them into custody." She went on to describe a tall, wavy-haired man with a droopy moustache, who had been seen sneaking in and out of the place for weeks. "The Mister Big, we reckon. They didn't get him, of course. They never do."

The description rang a bell – a bell that sounded all the way back to the abbey on the first night of his holiday.

"God, I can't believe you knew someone out of there."

"I can't believe it myself. But yes …"

"That's amazing. Hang on a minute." She flew inside and came out almost as quickly with the *Middlesbrough Evening Gazette*. "Look! Huh … how naff is that headline? 'The Birds Have Flown'."

Even in a moment of crisis, Kate Henderson-Pullar still had her journalism postgrad wits about her and corny headlines rankled. She positioned herself alongside him and held the paper across for him to see. Billy, never the brightest at comprehension, read haltingly and was hardly able to take it all in.

"See, they got five and the seedy little guy."

"I just missed her. Just missed her ..."

"What do you mean?"

"That Maria. I could have saved her."

"But you couldn't. You wouldn't have got past the door, believe me."

"I could have done something."

"Look, if I were you, I'd go over there right now and tell that policeman, if you really think this friend was one of them. I mean, it's heavy stuff."

"But I can't. My friend wants me to keep it quiet. She's kept like a prisoner. And she's still with ..."

The colour drained from Billy's cheeks. The place was raided yesterday. Luan had obviously avoided arrest. He was acting very strangely when Billy met Sofia outside the station. Did he already know something then?

"What time was the raid?"

"Afternoon. About two."

"Was there a white-haired girl amongst them? I mean very white."

"No. We saw them all. They looked East European. Very."

"I've got to get back. I've got to warn her. There isn't time to sort things out here."

"But it won't take you five minutes. It's the obvious thing to do."

"You don't understand. She's still with him and I don't know the address! I can tell the police in Whitby later and show them exactly where they're staying! There isn't time for me to mess about here. I've got to warn my friend right now, this afternoon!"

"Then ring her! Text her."

"I can't. She doesn't have a phone ... she doesn't have anything. Look, I've got to go ..."

He turned and was about to run off, when she grabbed hold of his arm.

"Maybe you're right, but wait a second!" She rushed inside again and brought out a vivid pink business card. "Here. Let me know what happens. I'll tell him over there that you've just been. You got a contact number?"

"No. I'm in a caravan. But you can have this ..."

He always kept Mother's mobile number in his wallet, written on the ripped-off end of a bus ticket. He handed it to her.

"And who is this?"

"It's my mother – Corinne Ingham. Please, if you can find out who was in there ... Her name is Maria Pladici." He took the small envelope from his body warmer and held it up for her to see. "See! That was the name. I was going to pass this on."

"Maria Pladici ..."

"If you ring, just say you have a message for William."

He turned to set off.

"Hey! You might need this!"

She handed him the newspaper. He snatched it ungraciously, rolled it into a tube and sped off down the street. She went straight up to her office, repeating over and over the name she'd just seen on the envelope. Billy had made an instant impression on her. Up to now, she'd had a low opinion of young men. She'd got lads' mags and tabloids banned from the union even before the bust – and that had reinforced her opinions even further.

She scribbled down everything she'd just heard and seen, then ran over to the policeman.

"Sorry to trouble you again, officer, but something odd has just happened. Something very odd ..."

Billy just made the 12.15. It was pulling out of the bay as he arrived. He darted onto the oil-stained tarmac and hammered his fists on the door furiously. The driver let him on, but had a face like thunder.

"You could've got yourself killed doing that."

The drive across the moors was picturesque torture. It seemed to take much longer than the journey there. Billy shifted about in his seat, turning things over and over in his mind. He kept taking out the rolled-up paper from his inside pocket to read again. Maria Pladici must be one of the arrested girls. Who else could it be? Billy was not that worldly-wise, but he eventually got the gist of the article. Luan wasn't importing cuddly toys.

The bus trundled into the outskirts of Whitby as if the world was still on holiday and nothing was urgent. The driver insisted on being friendly and helpful to everyone who got on and off. When they pulled into the station, Billy ignored the advice on the poster: Allow bus to stop before leaving seat. He stood with his nose to the door and jumped off even before the engine had juddered to a stop.

"You could've got yourself killed doing that an' all!" the driver shouted after him.

Billy dodged through the queues and out of the depot. He raced through the town and within minutes was at the end of the dilapidated terrace. He stopped dead at the front gate. He hadn't actually thought what to do when he got there! Throw a stone at the window? Go to the police first?

There was no time. He marched up to the door and let the lion-head brass knocker fall at full force. There was no answer. He knocked again, almost splitting the weather-bleached door in two. He stepped to the side and shaded his eyes. He peered into the gloomy front room. The debris was still piled high, but there was no sign of life. The 'birds had flown' here, too. They must have got wind of the situation in Middlesbrough.

Billy had failed at both ends. "But if I'd told the police there," he reasoned, "what could they have done anyway? It was already too late."

He talked out loud as if justifying himself to the world. He looked down at the step and recalled that moment he handed the handkerchief to Sofia.

"Should never have got involved ... always doing this, poking my nose in ..."

He made a mental note of the house number and the faded street sign. He trudged to the end of the tiny, forgotten staith, up the side street to a main street and then on to Crescent Avenue. He was in a daze ... it was as if he was sleepwalking. It took the roar of a refuse truck to snap him back into the present. He remembered Twiggy.

"The dog! Poor girl"

He was near exhaustion. Only the sense of duty quickened his step. It was still only two o'clock and he felt as if he had run a marathon through mud. He would see to the dog then, for what it was worth, he would go to the main police station in Whitby.

A chill autumn wind was blowing by the time he got to the caravan. The dog gave him a pathetic whimpering welcome that made him feel even guiltier. When she finally settled, he piled her bowl high with Tender Cuts and refilled her water dish to the brim. While she feasted, he cleared up the soiled newspapers and debris from the morning. He hooked her lead on ready to go to the police station. Gale-force winds were starting to buffet the sides of the van and it rocked alarmingly. He trudged wearily to his bedroom, discarded his ringing wet clothes onto the floor and slipped on a fresh T-shirt and trackies.

That done, he went to sit down for few moments' rest on the built-in lounge seat. He stared out of the bay window into Eskdale. Boats in the marina were bobbing up and down and straining at their moorings.

He shut his eyes and cast his mind back to the year before – the truancy, the break with his father, the promises he made to the grandparents. Here he was again, alone, in deep trouble and helpless. There was a girl out there in great danger, someone he had taken to in a big way, and he was utterly powerless ...

9

Long Shots and Long Snouts

Jayne Smith was something of a hero – eighteen months ago she was called to an armed robbery, got badly cut up – 'shanked'. She was awarded a medal, taken out of front-line service and promoted to desk sergeant. Now, she was practically office bound. Sometimes, she went out to talk road safety to schools; sometimes she did 'outreach' – trying to convince hoodies to see the police in a positive light.

"Like turning wolves into sheep," She said. After all, it was a hoodie who had shanked her.

She took a particular interest in women's issues. She'd had a rough time herself when she joined the force twenty years ago, mostly from fellow officers. So, one balmy July morning, when Kate Henderson-Pullar first came to the desk with her spiky hair and spiky attitude, she cottoned on quickly. PC Edmonds had turned away smirking, expecting to be regaled with some student issue or other.

"One for you I think, Sarge."

So it was and Sergeant Smith was more than interested. And what she heard that day led to an immediate investigation. Not long after came 'Operation Honeytrap'. The undercover boys were sent in – it was obvious what was going on – leading to the highly successful first of September raid.

When Kate Henderson-Pullar turned up again on the second of September, she assumed it was to say thank you on behalf of the world's oppressed.

"Ah, Ms Henderson!"

"Pullar ... yes, me again! It was me, sorry us, the Union ..."

"Yes, of course. Everything going all right?"

"Well, it seems to be."

She was well spoken. Her cultured voice and outrageous look did not quite match.

The Whitby Dancer

"Only seems to be?"

"Yes. I think there might be a bit of a sequel."

"Oh? I do like a good sequel."

"Probably not so good, I'm afraid. Your people are still there, of course, and it's being sorted, cool, but something odd happened this morning. I told them straight away, but they sent me up here to tell you. They seemed a bit dismissive."

"Did they now? They should have radioed in."

"I think they're fed up of me interfering. Anyway, this morning, I think it was about ten thirty, I saw a young lad …"

"A young lad?"

"Maybe sixteen … hanging around outside seventy-five. He looked worried – as if he was looking for someone there. When he came past our house, I told him what had gone on. It was obvious he wasn't a punter."

"That obvious?"

"Yes. He looked sort of old-fashioned and fresh faced. A nice kid, too."

"Maybe just curious. You know what people are like."

"No. It was more than that. He looked genuinely concerned."

"You spoke to him?"

"Yes. He said a friend had asked him to find out if another friend was living there."

"At that place? Confusing. Was he foreign?"

"No … English, very definitely, sort of Midlands accent. I should know. I was at school near Coventry. He really seemed to have no idea what the place was about. I mean really naive."

"So, let's get this straight. A young lad, English but not local, no name …"

"Oh, he said his name was Ingham … yes, leave a message for William Ingham."

"So, this William Ingham arrived at the scene of the investigation looking for a friend of a friend. And he seemed upset … and pretty genuine, too."

"Yes. I felt sorry for him. I said I'd find out if the friend was one of those you took away. I said I'd let him know, just to reassure him."

"Ah. So you have a contact number?"

"Yes; this. He said it was his mother's mobile. He seemed in a rush to get back. He didn't want to come here himself."

"Didn't he now? Did he tell you where he lived?"

"Well, he didn't say; he mentioned Whitby, I think."

"Hmm. So we just have a number …"

"Yes. He said he wanted to catch a bus and get back as soon as he could. So I gave him the article from *The Gazette*. He went white, I mean literally. Anyway, I said I'd find out what I could and let him know."

"Could be difficult. The girls are still being interviewed as we speak. They usually say very little until they feel safe. The pimps you see. They're still inside their heads and they'll stop at nothing. And, of course, hers is still at large …"

"Oh! He gave me a name. I wrote it down."

She slid an A4 pad over the desk.

"Maria Pladici …"

"That's the friend?"

"Yes, I think it is."

Sergeant Smith's brain was already ticking over. Some would pass off the story as irrelevant. But her intuition, twenty years worth of it, told her there was substance here.

"I'll see what I can do, Ms Henderson."

"Henderson-Pullar. You will chase it up, won't you? I felt concerned for him – I mean, they're ruthless those guys. He was only a kid. He shouldn't be mixed up with them."

"I'll see what I can do."

She turned to leave through the dingy foyer, but Sergeant Smith called her back.

"Your pad, Miss …."

Billy was woken by a frenzied hammering on the caravan door. It was gone three. He was so exhausted he had fallen fast asleep within seconds of sitting down. For the first time in weeks, the head injury was bothering him. He felt dizzy and nauseous. Twiggy was going berserk. He'd left the latch on rather than lock the door, so no one could get in while he cleared up.

It was Mother and Terry. She was furious.

"William! What on earth have you been getting up to now?"

"Up to? Nothing. What do you mean?"

"I got a phone call an hour ago! Yes. At two o'clock, to be precise. And do you know who it was from, William?"

The Whitby Dancer

He shook his head, but knew what was coming.

"Only the police. The police from Middlesbrough!"

"Oh ... really?"

"Yes, really. But we were supposed to be hiking to Robin Hood's Bay today, weren't we, William?"

"Yes ..."

"Then what's with the Middlesbrough bit?"

"Er ... last-minute decision. I was looking up Robin Hood's Bay in the library and picked up this guide, by chance. I fancied seeing the ... er ... bridge ... thingy ..."

"Transporter bridge."

Terry spoke pedantically, even in the eye of a storm.

"So you went there on a whim. Blown there by fate. To see a bridge. Then what's all this about you having a girlfriend?"

"I don't have a girlfriend."

"OK, a friend who is a girl then."

"Sort of a friend."

"Sort of friend? There's no such thing as a 'sort of friend'. For once, please be straight with me! What the hell is this about?"

"I'd tell you if I could ..."

"I'll give you fair warning. They've told us about you turning up at a police bust, at a massage parlour in Middlesbrough! Do you know what a massage parlour is, William? Do you?"

"I think I do now."

He pointed at the newspaper spread on the lounge table.

"My son tied up with ... well, what do you think, Terry? Have you been visiting such places? My own son, a 16-year-old? We were having such a nice time. How could you do this to me?"

"I was trying to help someone I met at your festival."

"Met? How? Most of the time you went around with a face longer than your dog's and you wouldn't speak to anyone. I knew I couldn't trust you to be left alone. And who the hell is this mysterious friend you were seeing under our noses?"

"She's an Albanian."

"What? Am I hearing right?"

"A folk musician."

"A what?"

"A folk musician."

"Is she on the official list?" Terry asked.

"I certainly didn't book any Albanian folk musicians."

"No, no ... she and her friend came here for a job, but then the friend disappeared. Now her uncle's keeping her like a prisoner, but she found out that Maria –"

"Maria?"

"... the friend ... was at that place in Middlesbrough. That's why I went, because Sofia asked me to."

"Sofia? Sofia?"

Billy froze.

"Mother. Did they say if there was an Albanian girl amongst them?"

"Oh yes, William, they were most accommodating. Albanian, Moldovan, Romanian ... a veritable Cook's tour of tarts! They wanted to know all about you and me! And they want you to ring them immediately to tell them where this friend of yours happens to be staying. Another massage parlour, I suppose, and they want to know where Terry and me live. Can you believe it? What's it got to do with us? And then when you've done with your phone call to Middlesbrough police station, and it won't be a private one, not on my phone, we're going to have words about you running off the rails again. I mean, you've never shown any interest in girls. Never mind Albanian folk musicians! Nan did warn me, she did say you were easily led and unpredictable ... just like your father."

Billy was hearing, but not listening. He knew what he needed to know. Sofia was destined for the same fate as Maria, just in another seedy northern town somewhere. While Mother was sobbing and throwing herself into Terry's arms soap-style, he was being overtaken by the most improbable thought ever.

Mother gathered herself enough to thrust her phone at him peevishly.

"Here! Get it over with. Now!"

She held up a number scribbled on a Post-it for him to read. Billy punched in the numbers; his fingers were shaking.

"Hello. Can I speak to ..." He peered at the Post-it, "PC Grady?"

"DC, you idiot!" Mother hissed.

"Sorry, DC."

There was a fraught silence, only broken by more theatrical sobbing.

The Whitby Dancer

"Hello, William Ingham speaking ... Yes, sir, it was me. Yes, my mother's told me ... yes I've got the address now. It's Fotherby Terrace, number 11. It's at the very end ... it's on the west side, not that far from the bridge. Yes, I'll hold the line ..."

He could hear orders and quick-fire organisation going on at the other end of the line. Then DC Grady came back on and gave him a string of instructions in the same staccato way.

"Yes, the girl from college told me they were dangerous ... yes ... yes ... no, I won't ... no ... I'll stay here with my mother. Pardon ... Oh! The caravan site near the ruins ..."

"Clifftops!" Mother interjected.

"The Clifftops ... number twenty-three; right by the main office ... OK ... OK ... OK ... I'll stay there with them ..."

He ended the call with a final promise to stay put and handed back the phone. He thought for a moment and then said distractedly, "They're on their way, but it's too late ... too late."

"For what? What do you mean? William, what do you mean?"

As Billy was fending off awkward questions, a moorland and a city away Sergeant Smith was working feverishly at the very next desk to DC Grady. He slammed down the phone and reached for his coat. She got straight on to Whitby to inform them about a possible 'feeder'. It seems they had the ideal bridgehead for traffickers on their patch; a small but busy coastal town, where people come and go and are never really noticed. An immediate search warrant was necessary.

"And I mean immediate ..."

Meanwhile, Billy was making his own plans.

"I'm going to take Twiggy for a walk."

"You're not going anywhere. Not after this lot. You're grounded!"

"But I've done nothing wrong. Did the police say I was being arrested?"

"No, but they told me you should be under strict supervision until they have all the facts. William, I know what you got up to at Brandywell. They warned me you could be a bit headstrong, but I never expected anything like this. If we're going to repair the damage of the past, we've got to come clean with each other. You could start by telling us exactly what you've got involved with. I mean, for God's sake, massage parlours ..."

"You just won't have it, will you? I'm going to my room."

"William, how the hell did you get involved with Albanians ... girls?"

"I've tried to explain, but you don't believe me. What else can I say?"

He squeezed past Terry and walked with deliberate calm down the corridor and into his room. He whistled for Twiggy who'd been watching proceedings nervously from her basket. She scurried after him and jumped onto the end of the bed. He began rummaging around looking for something, placing things gently out of the way, until he found what he wanted. He scooped the dog up and wedged her under his arm. Then he tiptoed to the half-open door and peeped out. They were at the far end of the corridor arguing. He sprinted out, pushed past Terry like a prop and then skipped round Mother like a fly half. He was down the steps before they could react. He tore down the service road with Twiggy under one arm and his body warmer under the other.

"Terry do something ... he's run off."

"I can see that!"

"You just stood there."

"What could I do? It's not for me to interfere. It's not my kid, is it? Bloody delinquent."

His instinct for parenting was even less developed than hers.

"We're supposed to be supervising him!"

"Correction. You are supposed to be supervising him."

"For God's sake!"

"I'm a folk musician, not a social worker."

Mother, still in the brand new moccasins she'd bought that morning, limped down the steps. Terry lumbered behind, cursing in broadest Geordie. He could dance the morris like an elf, but had no talent at all for running.

By the time Billy arrived at Fotherby Terrace, the inevitable blue-and-white tape was already in place. The police had made a forced entry. The rotten door was riven off its hinges and leant against the wall to one side. A constable, still as a Tussaud's waxwork, was on guard duty. Billy skidded to a halt.

"Can I help you, sir?"

"Officer. I'm the person who went to Middlesbrough."

"Were you now?"

"Yes. William Ingham. They were just on the phone to me. I'm supposed to see you."

The Whitby Dancer

The officer reached into his pocket and flipped open his notepad.
"Mr Ingham. William, you say."
"Yes."
"Aha! Weren't they expecting you to see you at ... er ... let me see ... at the caravan site?"
"Oh! I thought they meant here."
"And aren't you supposed to be with your parents?"
"They're on their way. They thought Mr Grady meant us to come here."
"No matter. DC Grady will need to speak to you all in a while. Perhaps you could wait in the patrol car up the way. I'll have a word with the officer."

He took out his radio, but Billy ducked under the tape stretched across the gateway.
"Whoa ... whoa ... you can't come in here. You'll contaminate the evidence."

He started to push Billy back up the path with his forearm. Twiggy growled.
"But they said I had to speak to the detective here."
"Not right now. And certainly not here. Wait up by the car."
"But there isn't time to waste. She's been taken off ..."
"She?"
"Sofia Zander. My friend who sent me to Middlesbrough!"
"Sanders ..."
"Zander with a Z."
"Of course." PC Irwell decided to spot-read the notes over again. "Yes ... Sofia Zander, second cousin of Maria Pladici ... native of Albania ... resident ..."

While he was occupied, Billy feigned a trip. By this means, he propelled Twiggy down the short path and into the doorway. She scrambled straight upstairs to the soulless woodchip room, where Sofia had been kept a virtual prisoner. A crime-scene investigator was dusting fingerprint powder onto a cheap, plywood dressing table. Twiggy burrowed past him and started to snuffle frenziedly around the bed.
"What the hell?"

He dropped his fine brush, ripped off his plastic gloves and lunged at her. He got hold of the upright stump of her tail and dragged her backwards down the stairs. She squirmed and snapped as he wrestled

Long Shots and Long Snouts

her along the corridor to PC Irwell. He, in turn, dragged her by the scruff of the neck along the path. Billy reached under the tape and grabbed her collar. It was like pass the mongrel.

"Bad girl! Really sorry about that."

"Please. Just wait at the end of the terrace until we're done …"

Billy retreated into the lane some yards away. He slipped his body warmer off and ordered the dog to sit. Then he opened out a broad side pocket and inserted Twiggy's long snout into it. She quivered and breathed deeply … PC Irwell watched incredulously.

It was the same pocket Billy had kept the fragrant handkerchief in. Twiggy was primed to hunt again, like she never had before. She tugged on the lead so hard, she pulled Billy off balance.

"Wait here, young man! We need to …"

As they keeled round the corner, Mother was arriving. A few seconds after, Terry hove into view red-faced and livid. He collapsed onto the flint stone wall of the house next door and mopped his brow with the bottom of his T-shirt. The look on his face said it all. All three exchanged querulous glances.

"Is it the boy Ingham you're after?"

"I'm afraid so, Officer. We did try to keep him in," Mother said.

"Did he say where he was going?"

"No. He raced off down towards the harbour. His dog ran riot in here. You must be his parents."

"She is, not me," Terry said between scouring breaths.

"Yes. I'm his mother. I'm so sorry he's causing you such trouble."

"Trouble? From what I can gather, it seems he's done us an almighty favour. They were up to no good in here. Syringes, fake documents, foreign currency, the lot. Seems it was a safe house for traffickers."

"So it's all true."

"We're seeing more and more of it these days. Even in the backwaters."

"So he could really be in danger."

"I don't think that for one minute. Not now, madam. There are plenty of loose ends to tie up and it seems he might be able to help, but that's all. It's only a matter of information – he's in no trouble himself, let me reassure you."

"I'm so glad you said that" Mother said. "… but what's he up to now?"

"He didn't say, but he did try to get in here! I'll put out a call. He can't get far ..."

"To the harbour you say?"

"Well, that way ... down the hill."

"We'll bring him straight back for the interview. Terry! Are you coming?"

"The man said he's putting out a call for him. Let them do it that's paid to do it."

"It's my son we're talking about!"

"He said there isn't a problem, so why the panic?"

She ignored him and careered off, the impractical footwear flapping against her heels. Terry slapped his hands down onto his knees in resignation, pushed himself up and lumbered off. PC Irwell radioed in to report the latest development and to alert any available cars to be on the lookout.

10

It All Comes Out In the Wash

Twiggy picked up the scent and Billy's sense of urgency. She pulled him chaotically from side to side, past the broad shop frontages in Flowergate. A postwoman was upended by the flailing lead – her neat bundle of letters skidding down the tarmac slope by Woolworths. There was no time to put things right. Billy shouted "Sorry!" and pushed on through a wall bank queue. He swerved round the steep, twisting corner at the bottom of the lane and, without looking, he cut diagonally across Baxtergate, the busiest road in town. A bus driver braked hard and blasted his horn. The trail was leading them on to the swing bridge and into the throng that squeezed through its bottleneck. They raced on relentlessly. This time, day-trippers had to move off the pavement for them.

As they reached the other side, an exuberant group of pensioners on the heritage trail were spilling across the road. Twiggy's nose was forced off the ground. She was patted and fussed until she was utterly confused. They were swept helplessly along to the end of Grape Lane, where Billy just managed to jerk her out of the slipstream and into a gift shop doorway. The chattering mob moved on. Twiggy reared up on her hind legs, raised her nose high and sniffed the air. She was waiting for a word or a sign. Billy took off his body warmer, held her by the collar and thrust her nose into the pocket again. She snuffled hard, but when he put the warmer back on, she remained absolutely still. There was only one thing for it – they retraced their steps all the way to the bank at the bottom of Flowergate and picked up the scent. Across the bridge, over the road, along the narrow bridge path … they painstakingly tracked back to the same point a second time. But Twiggy hit a brick wall again.

"Come on, girl, try!"

The Whitby Dancer

He led her off, but she simply tugged him up one side of Grape Lane and down the other. The scent was well and truly scrambled. There was no way forwards. Any minute now, either Mother or the police or both would appear. Billy slumped against a bollard and hung his head in despair.

"Are you all right, young man?" a passing traffic warden asked.

"I knew it was another long shot! Not meant to be this time ..."

The warden walked on with a puzzled frown.

Twiggy lay down by his feet; she had given up the chase entirely. There really was nothing left to do but go to the caravan, deposit her then face the music at the police station.

Billy set off along Church Street, rehearsing in his mind what he would say. They followed the long sweep of the Esk disconsolately. Soon, they were opposite the broad platform of the Endeavour Wharf. It jutted out into the river opposite and seemed much closer than it actually was. Billy stopped for a second and looked over – morris sides were dancing there just a few days before. He had watched them in dread, knowing his turn was soon to come. It seemed an age ago now.

As he was reminiscing, the lead tensed up like a fishing line with a bite. For the first time since Bridge Street, Twiggy's nose was down again and her tail was up and quivering. She was back on the scent. She pulled away so hard her claws scratched on the tarmac. She dragged him along with grim determination, until they came to the metal-grilled gate of a private quay not far from the steps that led to Terry's. Double layers of tight mesh and razor wire at the top made it look impregnable. Twiggy tried to prod her snout under the bar at the bottom. It was locked. She whimpered and clawed in frustration.

Billy peered through the mesh at a long duckboard jetty. It stretched from the sloping marina wall into the estuary. Several yachts were moored on either side of it; mostly the 25-footers used by local anglers, boats too tatty for tourist trips. But there was one much larger vessel, a restored old coble, at the far end. A shaven-headed sea-dog type was emerging from the cabin. He had a cigarette in one hand and a bucket of bait in the other. He clambered awkwardly over the lifeline on to the jetty, spat into the water and strode towards them. He fumbled with a key in his enormous, ruddy hands and clanked the mortise lock open. Billy pulled Twiggy back to get out of his way.

"After summat, mate?"

"Can we have a quick look at the boats?"

"Can't you look from there? It's private. Can't you read?"

At that instant, Twiggy slipped her lead, brushed past his shins and raced towards an empty mooring. She stopped so sharply she almost somersaulted in. The scent had come to a dead end. She circled round and round, scraping at the planking. She howled at the space like a wolf howling at the moon.

"What the bloody hell is that up to?"

The man raised a fist. Each knuckle was tattooed with a tiny swastika.

"Sorry! Can I just get her?"

"Be bloody quick. We're sick of the types we're getting round here these days. That's why we have to lock up behind us every time. Never needed to before. I suppose you're summat to do with them foreigners?"

He pointed to a decrepit blue-and-white yacht. It was steering into the open water of the upper harbour, but struggling to avoid a sleek 35-footer. Her engine whined as she turned.

"Tosspot! Does it every time. I told him to watch for the currents. Sails like it's bumper cars. Bugger off to where you come from, mate!"

The man was getting more and more aggressive.

"They're nothing to do with us! Honest!"

Billy cornered Twiggy at the far end of the jetty. She was still being driven mad by the sudden disappearance of the scent. He grasped hold of her collar and tugged her back to the gate. The man was tensed, ready to defend himself. She snarled and snapped as Billy bundled her past him.

"Just let it try, mate!"

The gate was slammed shut behind them.

"Sorry, mister …"

"You will be if I see you again."

Billy raced back the way they'd just come, keeping his eyes firmly fixed on the yacht as she went. Gut instinct told him it must be them. It was heading towards the swing bridge, heading out to sea …

The mast was tall, maybe 30 foot – it was obvious which way she was going and the bridge would have to be opened to let her through. There was still time! But not much … and to do what? As he turned into Grape Lane, he lost sight of the river. He tried to catch a glimpse down the passageways, but the Cook Museum, the antique shops and the

The Whitby Dancer

gallery were one solid block. He was trying to think on the hoof ... what the hell could he do? They turned into Bridge Street. Now the yacht was back in his sights, but the operator was already striding down the middle of the road, clearing the bridge of pedestrians. Lights were flashing and sirens were sounding like at a railway crossing. Soon, the barrier gates would be drawn across.

"If I can just get on it, get to the centre, shout a warning, cause a fuss ... Yes, that's it ... I can keep them bottled up until the police arrive."

He picked up Twiggy and marched to the gate, bold as brass. The operator was swinging it shut and was in no mood for banter. He was the real jobsworth, with the corporation donkey jacket and mission statement for a brain.

"Boat coming through! Keep your hands off, please. Move away! Move away from there!"

"Excuse me, can I have a word? It's urgent – that yacht there, it's ..."

Before Billy could explain, he clicked the drop latch down, turned his back and was striding away to attend to the other side.

"You've got to stop that yacht going through!"

The man looked at him as if he were mad. He locked off the far barrier. Billy couldn't get to the police now even if he wanted to. He could see the yacht's crosstrees through a tangle of stanchions and masts. It was positioned near the midpoint, ready to come through. Twiggy was squirming ferociously under his arm. He had to put her down. She started barking and leaping vertically up to the top rail. The operator was livid. He bawled at them in an irate, falsetto voice.

"Clear the gate please! Get your bloody dog away from there!"

"The dog ... that's it ... the bloody scrawny dog!"

It came to him in a flash. Terry's dinghy was a stone's throw away. Wasn't it right on the beach past Tate Hill Pier? Didn't he say he was keeping it there until he had a proper mooring?

Billy caught Twiggy mid flight. By now, the bridge master was keeping a close eye on them. He shook his head and tut-tutted as Billy stepped back from the gate.

"Good riddance ... everyone knows the score here ..."

Billy scurried around the corner on to the slippery cobbles of Sandgate. He barged his way through the slow-moving crowds browsing round the market bandstand then sped along the curved terrace of Tate Hill. He was almost there – Henrietta Street which ran, he remembered, exactly parallel to the harbour wall. He skidded headlong into Ted Morris' alleyway and raced past his door to the end of the row. He threw Twiggy on to the beach ahead of him then jumped off the tide-battered sea wall. His hunch proved right. The *Dog* was still there.

Sand kicked up behind them as they scrambled towards her. Billy lifted Twiggy into the bow.

"Stay there, girl! Stay!"

It was a good 20 metres from the shore. There was nothing else to do but drag it inch by inch. He gripped either side of the prow and pulled – his arms tensed and his back flexed like in a tug of war. With every heave, a deep groove was carved into the sand. Sweat rolled off the end of his nose. He had to go on. The traffic had come to a halt at each end of the bridge and people were gathering along the pier road to watch it in operation. With one final heave, he got the dinghy to the water's edge. He ran astern and pushed a final time. Where the sand was wet and shiny, it slid along so easily he fell flat on his face. He picked himself up and vaulted in over the port side. The oars were still wedged under the seat where Terry had left them. He took up the nearest and lanced it hard into the sand. They slipped sideways into the surf. He pushed again, using the oar as a punt, until they were fully afloat. Gentle waves lifted her into life … but now she began to list from side to side.

He drew the oar in, dropped it into the port side rowlock and sat on the plank seat to steady himself. He dragged the other oar off the deck with his spare hand and fumbled it into place. The bridge was drifting into view. A chink of light revealed it was being opened. He could just see a sliver of Eskdale and the crosstrees of the blue-and-white yacht swaying. Twiggy yapped hysterically; she knew when a chase was on. Billy started to row with a series of irregular dips and pulls, but it was by the sheer strength of his prop forward hands that he moved at all. He quickly worked out how to steer – a little less frequent one side, a little more frequent the other and she went roughly where he wanted. Somehow, he managed to dog-leg round Tate Hill and towards the fish pier. Critical eyes were beginning to notice, beginning to follow his ungainly progress. A knot of people were gathering around the lifeboat station.

The bridge hove fully into view – it was wide open. Now he could see the whole of the yacht and hear the diesel engine being revved into action – she was coming through. Billy edged farther and farther out. He was heading directly towards the main channel. The yacht's pulpit reared up and down as she hit the heavier swell of the lower harbour. Billy slid out the port side oar and pulled furiously with the other. He veered round in a semicircle, so he was aiming straight at them. He had to keep craning round to keep his bearings ... his barely-healed neck muscles were being torn apart again. Just one more pull, one more pull ... then he saw him! The sinister figure of Luan, hunched over the wheel, still dressed in a Savile Row suit and silk tie, still smoking nonchalantly. Billy pulled yet harder and craned round again. The pain was excruciating, but now he could see Sofia clinging to the starboard lifeline. Her head was hanging over the side and her hair was blowing wild. Billy was 30 metres ahead of them and closing. Now was his chance. He stood up and shouted, but the dinghy pitched and threw him back onto the seat. He gripped the gunnels tight and stood again. This time, he spread his feet wide and lodged his calves against the seat. He shouted again until his voice cracked ...

"Sofia! Sofia. It's me, Billy! Billy Ingham!"

He picked up an oar and swung it round his head, but the yacht ploughed on as if he wasn't there. Sofia still hadn't noticed. He would have to get even closer. He sat down, dropped in the oars and started to row again – harder, faster, until his wrists were cramping. Only when the *Dog* was a 10 foolhardy metres away did Luan realise ... some idiot was aiming their boat straight at him. He steered wildly to starboard, but the sudden surge threw Sofia onto the deck. At last, she was alerted. She saw him – and could hardly believe it was the young man who'd tried to help her. She gasped in amazement and stumbled to her feet, grabbed the line with one hand and started waving with the other.

"Sofia! You've got to get away from him! He's a trafficker ... he's ... he's ... no good!"

Luan threw his cigarillo at her and shook his fist furiously. Billy braced his legs and gripped the oars tight. The tide was forcing him towards the Scotch Head Bandstand; the yacht was arcing round him. He rowed with almighty gut-wrenching pulls, strained and strained, until his chest burned and the veins stood out in his neck. Now, Sofia was grappling with Luan; she was trying to slow him down. But Luan pushed her away and wrestled the wheel back under control. Billy was closing in, drawing alongside! He could hear Sofia screaming and Luan cursing. There were no more than 5 metres between them! The swell shifted and forced them even closer, so close they were going to collide! Billy let the starboard oar fall into the sea and reached out a hand. Sofia reached out to him ... their fingertips almost touched ... but then she was gone ... they were past him, sweeping rapidly away. Their wash was tipping him into the sea. Billy grabbed the port gunnel and swayed hard to right her. Water was up to his waist. Twiggy was paddling frenziedly. Luan was laughing like a maniac and gesturing a crude goodbye. They were almost at the harbour mouth and into free water. Billy sprang to his feet, braced himself one more time, took up the remaining oar, aimed it like a harpoon and thrust it towards them. He recoiled onto the seat. There was an almighty crack, then a metallic crash, then a splintering of wood. He dragged himself up to the bow. The dinghy was sinking. He had lost all control, but he could just see the oar sticking up from their stern, lodged between the rotor blades and the rudder. It had wedged tight. The engine screamed. Splinters flew out of the bubbling water, but the oar held firm. Luan was shouting, revving the engine to full throttle, but the steering was disabled; she was circling round Billy. The more Luan revved, the more the swell increased until he was thrown off the wheel. Centrifugal force pinned him to the lifeline. He was utterly helpless. On every tantalising circuit he glimpsed the North Sea and cursed to high heaven.

By now, the inshore lifeboat was scrambling. The crew were throwing on life jackets and clipping gear to their belts as they scurried along; one old salt said he'd seen nothing like it since the war.

"A torpedo jammed the Bismarck's rudder ... she circled like that until we sank 'er."

The dinghy bobbed and spun like flotsam in a whirlpool. It lurched a final time and capsized. Billy tried to grab Twiggy, but was tossed into the water as if thrown by a giant wrestler. He hit the surface so hard he swallowed brine. The sky, the sea, the harbour, the bridge swirled around like in a nightmare. Then everything went cold, quiet and grey ... something vivid black-and-white spun past his eyes. He tried to grab it, but it fell away into the gloom, spinning ... spinning ... ever smaller ... until it was gone. He was falling ... the grey became darker, denser, until it was pitch-black ... the blackness was everything. He was being sucked down, claimed, crushed. He felt numb ... powerless ... heavy, so heavy, so weary, he gave himself up to it. Nothing he could do ... all

The Whitby Dancer

darkness ... down ... down ... but then he was being magically lifted, buoyed up ... up ... The swell that had rolled him under was churning him up ... up ... from black to grey to green. He popped out like a cork into a brilliant, blinding light. He gulped a mix of sweet air and salt water ... then, by instinct, he broke into an ungainly doggy paddle.

He remembered little of what happened next. Just the feeling of wet sand giving way under his feet. And falling on to sharp, freezing shingle. A circle of faces was leaning over him ... a siren wailed in the distance ... then his senses closed down ...

11

Circles and CGIs

Billy woke up in the A & E of Whitby Hospital. A nurse was hooking a file to the end of his bed. His first thought was Twiggy.

"Is my dog all right?"

"The dog's in fine fettle. Your mother's taking care of him."

"You're not just saying that?"

"Cross my heart." The nurse was naturally jolly and very Northern Irish. "You've had quite an adventure, so you have."

The back of his head was sore again and the old dizziness was on him like the return of a curse. Was this the déjà vu Mother was always going on about? He struggled to sit up and look around, but flopped back on to the pillow, right onto the old wound. He winced.

"You be careful!" The nurse came closer to observe his reactions. "So you know where you are?"

"Hospital ... again. And I'm Billy Ingham and my phone number's ..."

"I get the point, young man. But we'll need to do some wee tests, so we will. We know you're physically in good shape – you've got the pulse of a pit pony. But your Mother told us about your wee bump and your whiplash, so we've faxed through to Shirlington General, just to be sure."

"Does this mean I've got to go through all that stuff again?"

"Stuff? You mean the lights shined in your eyes, the pokings and the proddings. Ha! Ha! More than likely, young fella!"

"But I've got things to do! There's no time ..."

"Things to do, indeed. Do you know how long you've been here?" He looked at his wrist. His watch was gone. "That'll be somewhere at the bottom of the North Sea, I expect. You've been out of it for two hours. Now ... arm please."

"I'm fine I really am!"

The nurse laughed. "That's what Nelson said before he died. You might have a secondary aggravation. Until we're sure your GCI's

The Whitby Dancer

normal ..." She pumped up the blood pressure unit until it was tight round his arm. "Good. See ... it's better than mine, so it is."

It hissed as it deflated. She detached it, noted the result and sped off down the corridor.

Billy was left alone in the cavernous silence, trying to gather his thoughts. It crossed his mind to get up. Only then did he realise he was naked, apart from a surgical smock. There was no sign of his clothes. There was nothing to do but listen to the pigeons scuffling round on the window ledge and the faint sounds of work and gossip echoing down the corridor. It must have been another hour before anything else happened.

Heavy, slow footsteps were drawing near. He could hear the sonorous tones of an officious man. Someone turned into the bay. Billy cringed. It was the same PC who was guarding the house where Sofia lived. The nurse was walking beside him, shaking her head.

"Yes. I fully understand, but if the lad could just clear up a couple of things, it would help us and, more to the point, his lady friend. We have to move quickly on this one, top priority government stuff."

The nurse wasn't convinced.

"The doctor wanted to have another wee look at him this evening. I can't let you loose on him until we're sure."

Billy listened with alarm. It was exactly the same scenario as at Shirlington and he wanted to be out of Whitby in exactly the same way. This time, he would take control, or as much control as he could whilst lying prone on his back.

"Hello, nurse ... I'm fine to see him, honestly."

"Hear that? The lad says he's fine."

"I'm not deaf."

"Come on. It really is just a five minute job. Nothing too involved. If anything goes wrong I'll take the consequences."

To Billy's relief, the nurse caved in.

"Be it on your own head. But I'll have to be in attendance."

Billy took a deep breath and pulled himself together. Head injury, hospital, police interview, identikit bobby – it was déjà vu to the power of ten. PC Irwell came close to the bedside with notepad at the ready.

"We meet again."

"My dog – she is all right, isn't she?"

The policeman assured him that Twiggy scrambled ashore in one uncontrollable piece.

"She made life so difficult for the medics they let her go with you in the ambulance. Highly irregular."

"I thought I saw her sinking. I thought she was drowned."

"She's in fine fettle. Safely back at your caravan, I believe. Now, I'm only going to take a brief statement from you. The detective will go into more detail about the main investigation later. This is just to tie things up regarding the incident in the harbour."

"Just you wait a minute!" The nurse interjected. She hurried off to buy them each a coffee from the machine along the corridor. "There. Take your time, Billy – don't let him bully you!"

She stood to one side with her arms folded and watched, and sometimes scowled. In between sips, Billy explained how he had met the girl, how he had promised to help her, how he had gone to Middlesbrough to find her friend and how he had rushed back to warn her. But she had gone. He only took the dinghy as a last resort.

"Piracy on the high seas ... very serious," PC Irwell joked.

"It was the only thing I could do to try and stop them."

"Not true. You could have notified us. I mean, we are the police."

There was a silence while Billy considered if it was worth trying to explain. For the sake of ease, he decided it wasn't.

"I'm really sorry about that. Is Sofia all right?"

"As far as I know, yes. Apparently, there was a decommissioned fishing boat a mile out at sea waiting to take them further south. Hull, we reckon. It's a sorry business. But she's had a check-up and she's fine."

"And her uncle?"

"Her uncle? He's being well looked after."

As the story unfolded, it was obvious to PC Irwell that William Ingham and Sofia Zander were singing from exactly the same hymn sheet.

"You stumbled into a hornet's nest," He said. "If that Albanian villain had been any stricter, you'd never have made the connection."

"He was strict. He only let her out once a day to do jobs. It was only because Twiggy tracked her after the dancing that I found out anything at all."

"Dancing?"

"That's when we saw her watching us at the morris dance. You know, the folk festival? She was upset and dropped a handkerchief."

"So yesterday was the second time you got the scent from that!"

"Well, that and the room."

"Ah yes. The room. Did I have egg on my face. Makes Lassie look like an amateur, that dog of yours. What's that medal they give to animals?"

"I haven't a clue," The nurse said as she was looking nervously along the corridor, "I've no time for quizzes. Or fairy tales for that matter. Are you done?"

"Nearly. I don't suppose he can give us a very brief written statement? Just about the boat, I mean. He can save the dance stuff for DC Grady."

"Absolutely not. He'll need to rest now, poor wee fella," she said. "I don't care if the Home Office itself is waiting on him."

"Just checking! Thank you, Billy. That's a good help. The fog's starting to lift."

"Oh, please, Officer, before you go ... I was wondering ... what happened after I was sunk?"

"The coastguard boys had to shout instructions at Zander through a megaphone to get him to cut the engine. He had to crawl on all fours to manage it. He'd still be out there now. That was another damn clever trick you pulled. You should audition for James Bond."

Billy didn't like to admit it was sheer luck born of desperation.

"Huh! To think – if you'd done as I told you yesterday or if your mother had caught up with you, we'd never have got him. End of story – oh, talking of stories, you'll be in the local rag I expect, son. They're milling round outside already."

"They won't be getting any statements, either!" the nurse said.

"Don't worry, I'll move them on. Now, if I could remind you, DC Grady will be with you later. If not here, at Clifftops first thing tomorrow."

"Clifftops tomorrow!" the nurse said emphatically.

"Yes, we won't trouble you again today. So no more gallivanting, Billy! Thanks, staff ..."

As he was leaving, fate decreed that Mother should be arriving. She passed PC Irwell with her eyes fixed firmly to the ground. The nurse saw her coming and quickly found something else to do in the ward office.

"William! Look at you all alone! Thank God you've come to. I thought you were going to drown. You were under for ages. Ages! Terry had to hold me back from diving in."

Mother was already rewriting history ...

"You mean you saw it?"

"Everything. I didn't want to believe it was you, but the dog confirmed it. It just had to be you, didn't it? Typical of my luck. Terry broke down when you sank. I've never seen a man cry like that."

Billy thought he'd better get off the subject.

"I don't really know why I'm being kept here."

She burst into tears.

"For heaven's sake, Mother, I'm feeling brilliant."

"It's not that, William …"

She struggled to talk through the blubbering. "It's Terry. He was so angry about his boat. I thought he was going to have a heart attack. He just stood there in total shock. 'It's only an old dinghy,' I said, to make him feel better, but he wouldn't speak to me. And then he wouldn't come to the hospital. He stormed off. And I followed on to see if he was OK and he slammed the door in my face. Slammed the door in my face! William … I think it's over between us."

That is a shame, Billy thought.

And the *Scrawny Dog* was still at the bottom of the main channel of the lower harbour. Like Mother's relationship, it was well and truly sunk.

Soon after Billy's brief statement was received, DC Grady took Sofia's full written statement at Whitby Police Station. She was slightly bruised and still a little damp, but she was more than willing to talk. There was no need for an interpreter – she spoke better English than many an English GCSE student. The case was unusually clear-cut. The lad in hospital was patently telling the truth. Everything was corroborated to the last splinter. A dropped handkerchief had led to the cracking of a human trafficking ring.

"You could write a book about this," DC Grady commented.

He quickly organised the information into his briefcase and set off to interview Luan Zander. He was already being detained in the police cell at Middlesbrough. The 'Honeytrap' team was quickly reassembled. The investigation was moving with untypical speed.

A duty social worker was called and Sofia was taken to a women's hostel. It struck everyone who dealt with her that she was remarkably together, considering what she'd been through. No one thought to tell Billy where she was.

Luan, meanwhile, demanded this right and that, demanded an interpreter, a lawyer, fresh clothes, food ... He threatened Grady with the *ambasado*, tried anything to confuse the issue. He accused Mehmet of being the trafficker. Apparently, he was actually the heroic uncle come to rescue his unfortunate niece and her friend. Grady relayed to Mehmet what Luan was alleging. But Mehmet smelled the coffee. He opened up. It was all extra grist to the mill – there was enough evidence on the yacht alone to put nice Uncle Luan away for a very long time.

"The lad was lucky," a coastguard had said during the search. He found a Kalashnikov propped up in the hold and enough ammunition to start a small revolution. "If he could have got to this ..."

As news filtered through, Sergeant Smith grew smug. 'Honeytrap' hadn't just been down to a copper's sixth sense. She did the research, kept one step ahead. She pinned up cuttings on the noticeboard behind her desk; the current hot topics for any young PC who showed an interest. There was one prophetic cutting, still not yellowed, that was circled with a red marker pen – sergeant's code for 'I told you so'. It was a *Times* article about people traffickers from Eastern Europe. Under-aged girls fetched a high price on the market. Exactly 200 years after Wilberforce's famous anti-slavery bill, they were being bought and sold like merchandise. Middlesbrough, it seemed, had a particular liking for them. PC Edmonds, her hard-bitten colleague, joked it was because there were no virgins left in this part of the world. Sergeant Smith didn't laugh.

Maria Pladici was deeply traumatised. But at least now that she was safe in the hospital and Luan was behind bars, it was confidently expected she would 'sing like a canary'. They would have to work fast. She wouldn't be in the country long. Another recently pinned-up cutting told how The Council of Europe had hammered out a convention, in which victims would be given sanctuary, time, counselling, support ... only the UK had not yet signed up to it.

"They're expected to stand on their own two feet, pull themselves together and go back to their own country as soon as bloody possible," Smith said to Edmonds, "... no matter that it's English punters who've been merrily abusing them."

* * *

Later that evening, Billy was moved out of the draughty reception ward. Despite his protestations, he was manoeuvred into a wheelchair by Mother and a 'rushed-off-me-feet' porter and pushed to a main ward. They passed by a dim-lit TV room. Some patients were arguing over whether to watch *The X-Factor* or *Strictly Come Dancing*. Billy winced. Mother stopped at the service desk to ring home. A nurse, preoccupied with paperwork, slid the phone towards her without looking up.

"Peggy, brace yourself. You're not going to believe this, but William's in hospital again. Yes, I said William is in hospital, for twenty-four hours' observation. Yes, twenty-four hours. He's bumped his head again ... what? No, in a fall from a boat. Yes, I did say boat ... aggravated something or other ... ridiculous, isn't it? No, I'm not joking. I wish I was ..."

After ten minutes of listening to Mother's garbled, oft-repeated account, the nurse glared up at her.

"I'll have to go!" Mother slammed the phone down. She was seething. "You'd think I'd hit you over the head with a baseball bat or something."

Nan was in shock. It took a moment or two to compose herself then she slipped her galoshes over her shoes and skirted round the muddy yard to the milking parlour. Grandad was barely halfway through the evening milking.

When Nan appeared at the large sliding doors he knew something was amiss. She rarely came over these days.

"It's Billy ... he's ended up in hospital again. Something about a blessed boat and people traffickers."

"What? People what?"

"Corinne didn't have time to explain. She was on the hospital phone. She says he's all right, but he might have exacerbated the wounds from the bike accident."

"I'll exacerbate his wounds when I see him. It's supposed to be a folk festival, all nicey-picey and bloody dancing round a maypole, not causing mayhem!"

"Well, don't judge before you know, John. I mean, it sounds like he's a bit of a hero."

"Hero? Boats? People traffickers? Am I hearing right?"

He carried on angrily thrusting suction tubes onto udders, while Nan filled in the remaining snippets of what she knew. It occurred to her it was exactly a year ago that Billy nearly drowned in the River Shirle.

"He seems to have a fatal fascination for water," she said.

"I think there's some kind of curse on us, Peg! It's Corinne and 'er blessed astrology! The sooner we send her packing the better."

"But it's nothing to do with her from what I can gather."

"Ah, well. So much for a bit of time to ourselves. I suppose I'd better pick him up first thing tomorrow."

"You can't. They're keeping him until three."

"Tyke will be happy!" Grandad stepped back to avoid a cow, irritated by a misplaced tube. "Look, I've gone to pieces! I expect he'll end up like his father. Then the fun'll really start."

Meanwhile, in Whitby, Mother was reporting back the latest arrangements.

"They'll be coming for you tomorrow afternoon."

"Who?"

"Grandad. Who do you think? Batman and Robin?"

Billy's heart sank. He wanted to see Sofia again, wanted to see things through to their bitter end. No one seemed to be listening to him. He was being treated like a lump of meat on a butcher's slab.

"Why can't I just go back to the caravan now and look after the dog? I'm feeling fine."

"William, they say your CGI –"

"I keep hearing that. What the hell is it?"

"Your Glasgow Coma Index ... it isn't quite normal. They've got to be sure you're not brain damaged! I suppose they know about things like that in Glasgow."

"But I've been answering questions, giving statements! I feel as if I could get out of bed and play a game of rugby now!"

"There's nothing I can do. I'm sorry, but you did get yourself into this."

"Everybody's blaming me, but all I did was return a handkerchief to a girl from Albania."

"Whatever you did, it wasn't exactly designed to help your mother. There'll be court cases and newspaper articles and what have you. I came home for the quiet life, not this."

Circles and CGIs

It didn't seem to impress her at all that her son was now a regular hero. Reporters were gathering at the entrance like hyenas.

"Huh. No wonder Terry's going off me. He's wondering what he let himself in for ... he'd only just got that boat. And he had commitments. I mean, couldn't you just have told the police a friend was in a spot of bother?"

"But I couldn't!"

"Why is there always so much melodrama with you, William?"

Billy could hardly believe what he was hearing. Melodrama? Him? That really was the ultimate in 'pot calling kettle black' statements.

"Anyway. I have to leave you now. I'm so busy sorting things out. William, you leave such a mess behind you."

"But what about Twiggy?"

"Well, since it looks like I'm staying at the caravan tonight, she'll have company. Even if it is only me."

"So it's definitely off?"

"I don't know ... I don't know ... I'm in a complete tailspin with all this ..."

She checked her watch, gave a pathetic little wave and was gone. It was obvious she was going to Terry's.

Billy slumped onto the pillows. The feeling of unfinished business haunted him. He could neither read nor sleep. He kept picturing the yacht getting away from him, Luan cursing and the last sight of Sofia as he sank beneath the waves. Yes. That probably was the last time he would ever see her. They had got so close, so fast. He'd never had such feelings before and here he was, in a waking nightmare. Helpless, ill, misunderstood ... disregarded ...

12

Mirupafshim and *Faleminderit*

There's something odd about Terry Thwaites. He's a man who likes a good story, a yarn or a legend. He'll sing you a traditional song about gypsies at the castle gate, brutal royal murders or illicit romance all on a summer's morn. He particularly likes a shanty, you know, drunken ribaldry, battling the trade winds, sailing into exile halfway round the world. He even writes his own songs about miner's strikes or shipping disasters. But when something of note actually happens to him ... something so dramatic it cries out for a song, a yarn or at least an anecdote, he doesn't want to know. He prefers his life experience by remote control. So, to him, 'The Famous Incident of Billy Ingham and the People Trafficker', a true-life adventure, featuring a chase on the high seas and a hint of romance, was unwelcome turbulence. Terry Thwaites was not inspired by it, he was infuriated. His performance dinghy was sunk and now threatened the main channel out of the harbour. It had cost a lot of money, borrowed money. Now, he had the hassle of salvage, even before the maiden voyage. He'd only had it three weeks. He hadn't got round to marine insurance. He hadn't even finished stencilling 'Scrawny Dog' on the bow yet. So when Corinne Ingham turned up at his doorstep late on Saturday night hoping to put things right between them, he was in no mood for amateur dramatics. Yes, he did let her in, but only to let her down.

"It's been a fantastic two weeks, Corinne, it really has. To quote Mike Harding, it was all 'good stuff'. But it can't go on. You live in the East Midlands ... and you're still in remission after your split. I've been through it myself, hinny ... got the T-shirt, got the beer belly ..."

She wasn't amused. She broke down in tears and threw herself on the Chesterfield, the soft, shiny leather Chesterfield that held so many memories.

"So I was just another groupie, was I?"

"Of course not! Who do you think I am, Mick Jagger? It's time to get back to reality, Corinne, and we both know it." He was the type who preferred to have his own space, his own time. "We can keep in touch. See you in the beer tent next year." He nudged her playfully and winked.

"The beer tent next year? Thank you so very much."

And so ended Corinne's romance. Goodbye to the fantasy of being a permanent folk chick, endlessly going to roots festivals, living on real ale and quiche salad from the food tent. It was over. And she blamed William, blamed the foolish, selfish, headstrong lad, who sought out trouble like a smart missile and left destruction in his wake.

She trudged back to the caravan the cliff top way. An autumn mist was drifting in off the sea. The half-moon glowed faint and seagulls squawked a lament. For all her faults, she was a genuine romantic: the dark cliffs, the abbey ruins, the toppled headstones in the graveyard; all seemed to be coming out in sympathy. She would have to go back to Brandywell the next day and throw herself on the mercy of the cantankerous old Inghams again. That stuck in her craw. She thought she had found happiness. She thought she had found a way out. Typical. It was too good to be true. As the song says, 'Back to life, back to reality'.

That night, the dog moped at one end of the caravan, she at the other. But she determined she would see Terry one last time. He couldn't mean all that stuff about 'space' and 'remission'. Before she went to the hospital in the morning, she would surrender utterly to his will. You just never know. She would even offer to buy him a new dinghy ... yes, William's insurance money would be coming through soon ...

The grandparents set off mid morning soon after Tyke arrived. The milking was done. Tyke only had to keep an eye on things until the tanker came. They planned to arrive exactly when Billy's twenty-four hour observation was due to end. They would give him advance warning, so he could get ready while they cleared the caravan.

Billy had the usual boring hospital day with the same old National Health routines and mind-numbing daytime TV. A genteel old man, sitting in the day lounge beside him, hit the nail on the head.

"If you're sick, the worst place to go is hospital."

Mirupafshim and Faleminderit

The doctor arrived at midday. It was immediately clear the mysterious GCI was AOK. A nurse followed soon after with the drugs trolley, which Billy happily refused. She gave him the familiar 'Head Injuries' card with symptoms to look out for. He read over it several times, simply because there was nothing else to do.

Not a single minute passed without him churning over the events of recent days. *A Lass from Richmond Hill* played over and over in his mind like a stuck CD. He kept reliving that fateful morris by the monument, finding the dropped hanky, the trip to Middlesbrough, the race back, the splintering oar in the rudder, the last sight of Sofia hanging onto the lifeline, Twiggy spinning into the void ... then nothing. It was as if a video had been frozen at that moment ... the story had no ending. At two, the message came through. He left the day room to pack his things into a carrier bag, then he sat on the bedside chair and waited ... and waited. The ward was half empty and deathly quiet.

A beam of light streamed down from a high window, showing up the dust floating around like plankton. He drifted in and out of daydreams ... he was somersaulting out of the boat ... sinking again ... then swimming ... then somersaulting ...

At ten to three, he was roused by a shake of the shoulder. It was Mother. She had a distant look in her eye and her voice was cold and mechanical.

"They're here, William. They're at the van now. They're picking us up in ten minutes. Are you ready?"

"Yeah. What about your stuff?"

Mother sniffed. Her eyes were red-ringed and smudged with mascara.

"He dumped it in the front yard. He didn't even open the door to me. Didn't even open the door ..."

"Oh. I'm sorry about that."

"Are you, William, are you really?"

With that, she excused herself and retreated to the Ladies to reconstruct her face. At that instant, Grandad breezed in.

"And what have you been up to this time, our Billy? Nan's bloody livid. People traffickers?"

Nan followed in, smiling benignly at patients like a visiting Queen Mother. She took hold of Billy's hand and squeezed it gently.

"The police rang early this morning and told us the whole story, Billy. It seems you're a bit of a hero."

"People keep saying that then ignore me!"

"Oh, I don't know about that. There was a man from *The Sun* at the entrance. 'Name your price', he said. Your Grandad sent him packing. We'll have none of that in our family! Not tabloids!"

"Where's your mother? Where is that woman now?" Grandad was indecently keen to get going.

"She's in there. A bit upset over Terry."

"Ah. She's been carrying on, hasn't she?"

"Yeah ... you may as well know ..."

"We know all about it. She was on the phone until the early hours. We're like the bloody Samaritans these days."

"I think it's all off, Grandad."

"Can we have that in writing?"

Grandad was almost as upset about the break-up as Mother. The prospect of her coming back to Brandywell filled him with dread.

Sergeant Smith wasn't on shift until Sunday evening, but she was eager to meet the feisty Albanian girl. She set off for Whitby at twelve, bringing sweets and flowers from the lads at the station and a message from Maria.

She was not in uniform, so she had to show her ID to a kind but overly-suspicious care worker before she was conducted to the visitor's room. It had the same sort of feeling as their police station foyer: sparse furniture, undecorated walls, a variety of stains, a single, gloomy Lowry print hanging over the mantelpiece. The care worker left the room. After a few minutes of footsteps padding up and down corridors, she returned with the girl. Sofia looked fatigued and frightened, but a proud spirit shone through.

"Hello. Sergeant Jayne Smith. You can relax ... it's not really an official visit."

She described, in exaggerated speech, what the situation was. Special Branch was having a final few words with Maria, but she could see her soon. She would be joining her in London, where the embassy had arranged accommodation for them. From there, they would be deported.

"Sorry! That sounds bad, doesn't it? You will be accompanied to the airport by your own embassy officials and you'll be met at the other end. Maria Theresa Airport in Tirana, I believe it is?"

"Yes."

"And your father will be there, too!"

At this, Sofia began to cry gently.

"Thank you so much ..."

"Did you know that Maria has agreed to give evidence?"

"Yes, I do know that."

"But that can be done via Interpol. There'll be no unnecessary delays. We'll get you home as soon as we can."

The testimonies of the other girls would be enough to convict Luan. They had been under his control much longer. Oddly, he had done nothing wrong to Sofia, apart from smuggling her into the country!

"All in all, Ms Zander, it's the happiest ending possible." Sergeant Smith spoke as cheerfully as her dour nature would allow. "Maria was lucky, you see. She managed to avoid the drugs and the diseases. Another week and who knows? Once they get them on the needle ..."

At this, Sofia broke down completely. She had only just come to understand the truth about Uncle Luan. She had not yet come to terms with it. She dreaded the thought of telling her father what had gone on. How stupid they had been. How evil Luan really was. He was always a character ... but this?

Sofia was pleased to meet the sergeant and grateful for the way she had been treated. But she was desperate to see her friend and to get back home. No more police, no more social workers, no ambassadors in London ... just get home, walk along the dusty path through the pine woods to the farm, see the sunlight glinting off the minaret in the village. The thought brought a smile to her lips, so she was crying and smiling at the same time. Sergeant Smith swallowed hard and looked away. She never gave way to emotion. She had a job to do, even though this was, strictly speaking, a personal visit.

"It won't be long, my dear. They'll pick you up tomorrow and you'll be home by Wednesday. Look, while I'm here, I'll have a word with a few people, try to move things along. I'm off down to the local police station. They said they might need to see you one last time ... couple of minor things ..." She was not usually given to displays of affection. But on this occasion, she moved forwards stiffly and put her arm around

Sofia's shoulder. "I'll pick you up in an hour or so. Get yourself ready and try to have a bite to eat ..."

Sergeant Smith made her way to the door, but Sofia stood up sharply.

"Oh! *Ju lutem! Ju lutem!*"

"Sorry – I don't ..."

"Please! Before you go ... there is one last thing ... one last thing to do!"

Grandad hobbled down the hospital steps and on to the car park. Nan was comforting Corinne. You would have thought it was her who was recovering from an accident. Billy was dragging his heels. He was still in the foyer, distancing himself from the scenes ahead.

Twiggy was in the back of the Land Rover. She spotted Grandad lumbering towards her and began the usual bounding up and down and high-pitched whining. It carried all the way to the hospital.

Billy emerged onto the steps groggily and surveyed the scene. It was an unappetising prospect: summer over; school looming; sore head; long journey to the Midlands; an even more neurotic Mother. No doubt Nan would be interrogating him. No doubt there would be more police enquiries on the horizon.

Then? The inevitable grounding and a very real chance of being moved on. Why was he always in trouble? Why was life so difficult?

By now, the others were in the car. Nan was beckoning Billy from the window, while Mother was fending off the dog in the back seat. Grandad was opening the door again and craning over the roof to see what the delay was.

"Come on, our Billy, get a shuffle on. I've got to get back for six! Tyke's playing doms in The Miller's Thumb at eight! I just daren't put on him any more."

Billy took a last look at Whitby, breathed in the salt air and then limped down the steps. He was about to cross the road, when a brand new Renault drew up. It braked harshly to a halt, ignoring the double yellow lines. The passenger door flung open. It was Sofia.

"Billy! Billy! My friend, it is you." She hugged him tightly. She hugged him and cried. "Billy ... Luan was such a bad man! Very bad!"

"Yes ... I know ..."

Mirupafshim and Faleminderit

"But you have saved me! *Faleminderit! Faleminderit!*" She hugged him again. "You so brave ... I never forget you ... I thought you were drowned ..."

He was too speechless to respond, too shocked to hug her back! He just stood there like a pantomime stooge.

The family watched from the car, silenced by the moment. Even Grandad knew they should not be interrupted.

"Billy, I have to go now. I have to go to London. Maria is waiting and we have to talk to officials. I will write you. I will get your address from polici and I will write you."

She hugged him a last time. Sergeant Smith got out of the car and took her arm.

"Come on, my dear. The inspector's waiting. It'll soon be over."

"Please ... I have to see little dog."

Billy pointed to the Land Rover. Sergeant Smith nodded, smiled and let her go. Sofia ran helter-skelter between the parked cars. Billy followed painfully slowly. Grandad wound a window halfway down.

"My, you are a pretty young lady," Nan said as she came near. "I can see why he was taken with you."

Twiggy pushed her nose through the half-open window and licked Sofia's face furiously, trying to squeeze through.

"I see you again one day! One day you meet my Kaji!"

Sergeant Smith had followed some paces behind. She took hold of her arm again.

"Ms Zander, please. We're on double yellows!"

Sofia accepted meekly. She unclasped her hands from Twiggy's face and turned away. She stood for a second and then waved a warm goodbye to those she'd only just met. Billy had arrived at her side and she kissed him on the cheek. He blushed.

"I never forget!"

Sergeant Smith conducted her back to the Renault, held the door open for her and then pushed it gently shut. Billy was rooted to the spot. He was aware of a car pulling away. He was aware of a girl's voice calling, "*Mirupafshim*, Billy ... *Mirupafshim!*"

But he was not really there. He was in the throes of a different kind of concussion ...

* * *

The Whitby Dancer

By the time they arrived home, it was almost seven. The journey was silent. A story needs time to sink in and each of them had quite a story.

As soon as they were through the door they went their separate ways. Nan put the radio on. Grandad went to the shippon. Corinne went up to the spare room to put on her Scrawny Dog CD. Billy pulled on his wellingtons and slung his binoculars round his neck.

He owed the dog a good, long walk. He let her race ahead. There was no call for a lead at Brandywell. She skipped over the cobbled yard to the end of the barn and down the long grass lane to the riverside. This was their favourite place on the farm ... the ring of ancient blue stones that skirted the River Shirle. There, the water meadows flood and dry in a natural cycle that leaves room for wildlife. Twiggy ran off to chase rabbits. Billy hauled himself up on to the flattest, lowest stone. He rested his head on the cool, hard surface and looked up. The swifts were hunting high, a last feast before the journey south. Their shrill, single cries pierced the evening stillness. A wisp of cloud drifted across the darkening sky – like a tousled mane of pure white hair.